I0727242

Professor Jack

MJ Politis

276 5th Avenue Suite 704 #944

New York, NY 10001

Copyright © 2025 MJ Politis

ISBN (Paperback) 978-1-80704-286-8

ISBN (Hardback) 978-1-80704-287-5

ISBN (eBook) 978-1-80704-285-1

All rights reserved

This novel is entirely a work of fiction. The names, characters and incidents portrayed in it are the work of the author's own imagination. Any resemblance to actual persons, living or dead, locations or events is purely coincidental.

No part of this publication may be reproduced, stored in a retrieval system, copied in any form or by any means, electronic, mechanical, photocopying, recording or otherwise transmitted without written permission from the publisher. You must not circulate this book in any format.

Cover Design by Woodbridge Publishers.

Find out more about our upcoming releases and authors at www.woodbridgepublishers.com and sign up for our newsletter to stay updated!

DEDICATION

ACKNOWLEDGEMENTS

ABOUT THE AUTHOR

Table of Contents

CHAPTER 1

"In or out?" Nathan Williams screamed out, his voice deep as James Earl Jones, his complexion twice as black.

"Huh?" the Gen-X drifter said from inside the doorway of the Last Chance Cafe, a rotting wooden fortress defiantly refusing to surrender to the elements.

"The wind. The bugs. They stay out there, I stay in here. That's the deal I made with this goddamn desert. In or out?"

"Okay, in," the drifter mumbled through a cynically indifferent frown.

Harry had been on the road for ten months, had used up at least twenty aliases, and had all of his money. He was a 17-year-old dropout, going on 50 faster than even he realized. Had it not been for the bus driver checking the toilets between stops, he would be in Las Vegas now, maybe even L.A. Younger Rapids, New Mexico, population 105, was the middle of nowhere, particularly to a kid whose images of the Old West were fed by Marlboro Billboards and Brat Pack Westerns.

The real West was a lot slower than in the movies. And a lot hotter, 100 degrees, and still mid-morning. And dry, too. The only thing Younger Rapids seemed to be flowing with was boredom, and Harry hated boredom most of all. But it was a change from the terror that had followed him from New York to Seattle and a thousand other places in between.

Harry had been in exile from even "alternative" mainstream life since he turned fifteen, acquiring powerful enemies on both sides of the ever-shifting line of legality. There were basically three laws to this new life without rules. First, keep your dreams alive. Second, be honest. Third, fill your stomach whenever you can. Harry had learned these rules at a dangerously slow rate.

"What'll you have?" Nathan asked.

"What do ya got?" The reflex response was abrupt, smartassed, and challenged a comeback.

"Lobster Newburg, Eggs Benedict, and Filet Mignon." Nathan threw Harry a list of generic truckstop options, a faded menu with prices crossed out and jacked up ten times since it was printed in 1962.

On first glance, Harry was not Nathan's kind of preferred customer. Though Harry didn't look like he was carrying a knife or a gun, he carried a more powerful weapon, a mirror. When you looked into his eyes, you saw yourself, whoever you were. If anyone was a James Dean for the 90s, without the paycheck, recognition, or record contract, it was Harry. A 98-pound bag of tattoo-covered bones. Shabby hair, which had been dyed more often than washed. Leather pants that reeked of sweat. And from behind the ten dollar sunglasses, the "look."

No one was going to give Harry shit anymore, maybe because he had a lifetime of it already. His mother died in a "domestic incident" two years earlier. His father, a crooked ex-cop now legitimate and crafty enough to work both sides of the law, beat the manslaughter rap. Harry's younger brother survived the domestic arguments and the physical abuse, only to end up in a string of mental hospitals. His sister had the good sense to leave home five years ago and the stubbornness not to let anyone know her whereabouts. There were many scores to be settled, and Harry made very powerful enemies after making some heavy-duty accusations. Still, he was determined to put things right, no matter who got hurt. But biological sustenance would have to come first.

"To start, a glass of hot water. Shaken, not stirred. And without any roach piss in it." All of the other ingredients were there. Catsup, mustard, crackers, salt, black pepper, and the red stuff in the dispenser, used to try to make pizza with American cheese taste Italian, for palates conditioned on the beans and bacon rodeo circuit.

Nathan returned the request with an uncompromising stare. He would have preferred a "please," or even "if you have time," but a quarter slammed on the table was enough compensation. "The minimum charge is usually two dollars. I'll let you decide what you want and be back later." Nathan laid it out.

"Yeah. Before the lunch rush."

Nathan took the quarter. The Last Chance Cafe would be a paying-customer-only establishment as long as Nathaniel Hawthorn Williams was in charge. There hadn't been any customers in for three days, but it was Nathan's place to know that, not Harry's.

With hot water and a tea saucer in hand, Harry went to work concocting his own, yet-to-be-patented recipe.

"One pack of mustard. Two hits of catsup. Pepper. Crackers aged a year past their expiration date. And two handfuls of sugar cause life to be so sweet when you're on the road. I'll call this one, artificial tomato surprise a la.."

Harry took out his worn-down two-inch pencil, grabbed a napkin, and turned to his host. "What's your name?"

"Sir, to you."

"Okay. Artificial tomato surprise a la Sir."

Nathan found himself softening. "You writing a book?"

"How to survive on the road on nothin' a day. It's gonna be a real money maker. But I gotta get some paper, and a publisher, and find a few million broke people who can pay three bucks a copy first. Details."

"So, you have a purpose. A dream," Nathan commented with admiration and envy.

"No. I have a family. One member I'm gonna see dead, or put away for good, this time. And two others whom I'm gonna find, then bring to Missoula, Montana. Or someplace else that's got animals, mountains, and a blues bar, in case I get homesick."

As Nathan cleaned the grill for the third time that morning, he noticed something intense in Harry's eyes. Something different, maybe. He knew enough not to ask any more details. He took out some frozen fries, the curly kind reserved for paying customers, two generous slabs of ham, and three grade AA eggs.

"Nathan," he said. "My name is Nathan. If I'm gonna be made famous, might as well get the name right."

"Nate. How 'bout Nate?" Harry countered, with the reflex insensitivity he used so often to defend himself against kind words from people he didn't yet trust.

"Nathan. My name is Nathan. And the breakfast special this morning is bacon, eggs, and fries. Five dollar value, special price today, two bucks."

"I'm puttin' down 'Nate'. It's my book. I'm gonna get rich my way, and I'll call this recipe whatever I want. Tomato-mustard-burnout's delight, a la Nate."

"You sound like you got 'youthful enthusiasm'. And you sound like you got some history behind you. You're probably a hungry motherfucker, too."

Harry reached into his pocket. A better find than he thought. "I got two quarters, three dimes, and a Canadian Loonie, worth a dollar if we were in Vancouver. Ya know . . . where all you 60's burnouts used to hang out. A cool place, 'til you all turned into losers or money gougers."

Nathan's black face turned beet red. "Breakfast special is two-fifty."

"You said it was two bucks."

"Price went up. Inflation."

No one was going to give Nathaniel Williams the "get a life" speech and get away with it. Nathan's hero in Vietnam was Jim Brown; his role model upon his return home to Watts was Martin Luther King; and his reality for the last decade, Al Bundy.

Harry proudly gulped down his burnout delight a la Nate, but his stomach churned, and he was still lightheaded. "Light-headed people make lots of mistakes and go weird real fast," he thought, remembering how chronic hunger was the first step downward on the spiral to getting your throat cut in an alley, or doing it yourself.

"So, Nathaniel, if I kiss your ass and tell you how great the 60's were, and how great a job you guys did for us, and how all us white guys really wanna get tight with you 'brothers', I get the breakfast special for a buck?"

"Three dollars." Nathan held firm.

Harry listened to his churning stomach again, then glanced down at a crucifix around his neck. The religious significance meant nothing. The fact that his mother gave it to him did. Harry ripped it off. His mother was dead anyway, as were his dreams of making something out of his life on his own terms. He emptied the last of his change and good luck on the table.

"The three dollar breakfast special, and your best house wine."

Nathan laid down the breakfast special, then a bottle of Lysol.

"Is this a joke, Nate?"

"No. Right now it's a statement of fact." Nathan gave back the crucifix, then the money. He turned away, too painfully aware of his own dead-ended existence to offer any explanations or life lessons.

Harry looked at the Lysol bottle, inverted a dust-stained glass, poured a generous portion, then lifted it up to his lips. As predicted, it caught Nathan's attention.

"You don't think I'll do it," Harry said.

From Nathan, silence and a blank stare.

"Tell you what, Nathan. If I drink this ammonia-scented house wine, you give me a hundred bucks."

"All I got is forty-two." Nathan put his money on the table. "And a check for the rest."

No one had taken Harry up on the bet before. "You don't think I'll do it, Nathan?" He took off his shades, his intense eyes behind them.

Nathan smiled. "You drink it fast, they take you to the morgue. You drink it slow, they take you to the mental hospital. You don't wanna be dead, kid. And I know you're not insane. Crazy, maybe, even visionary, but not insane. And those assholes in the rubber room motel don't know or wanna know the difference between insane, crazy, and visionary."

Nathan's logic was correct. But Harry's list of options was dwindling fast. He had fallen far behind on his timetable of settling the score with his father and reuniting his sister and brother in Montana. Each time he got up to take another step, life pushed him back another three. The harder he tried, the bleaker the prospect for any of his dreams.

"What's wrong with taking a one-way visit to the morgue?" Harry intervened. "I jammed with some good bands. No payin' gigs. Not yet. But I'm a good harp player. Carried lead guitar too, when Big Elmo got drunk and barfed his guts out in the alley, for the second set at the Golden Dollar. The crowd didn't even notice that he was gone. Dying's not so bad. How could I pass up a chance to jam with Hendrix, Morrison, even Jerry Garcia? A hell of a lot more bitchin' time on that side of the line than this one. Give me one real reason why I shouldn't take myself out now, instead of dying slowly like the rest of you."

Nathan remained silent. Harry became desperate.

"Come on. Tell me one good reason why I shouldn't off myself, right now!"

From out of a dark corner of the room, a voice crisp as a New England autumn day, "Because the bastards will have won."

His back was hunched and twisted, but he walked with steady, bold strides. His shoulder-length hair was gray, combed back over the top of a large bald spot. His jacket was corduroy, with leather patches on the sleeves. Around his stubby neck, a blue bandanna, held in place by a

Harvard fraternity ring. On his feet, traditional Apache moccasins, beaded in the manner of the Navajo. His face was baked tight and dry by the sun, his eyes coral blue and wide open. If the light hit him straight on, he looked like a well-seasoned multicultural guerrilla warrior in his forties. In shadows, he seemed to be an eighty-year-old ghost.

"Professor!!!" Nathan screamed out, apprehensively. "I thought you were still with them Hopi Indians."

"They're called First Nations People now. Not Indian," Harry countered.

"When you're as old as I am, and as old as those Hopi are, they're Indians." Nathan volleyed back.

The Professor sat down, trying not to let on that he still felt some pain when changing positions. Sitting was always more painful than standing for him, but his table was empty, and it was appropriate to watch what would happen from a sitting position this time.

"Indian?" Harry blasted out. "How would you like it if I called you Nigger?"

"I don't give a goddamn what you called me, as long as there's some respect behind it!!!" The button was pushed, and the wave of missiles was released. "I've been called Coon, Nigger, Darkie, Spook, and a thousand other names that you young bucks ain't even heard of. Of course, when you 'rediscover' them, they'll be 'cool' again. A real 'with it', 'hip' kinda language. You want to invent your own generation, invent your own language, motherfucker!!!"

"A loser and Nigger calling me a motherfucker? What the fuck is that?!! No one calls me a motherfucker!!!"

Nathan knew nothing about the reverence with which Harry held his deceased mother, but it was no excuse. Harry wouldn't be dissed like that. Personal honor demanded satisfaction, or blood.

"Motherfucker," the Professor quietly interjected, realizing that the next step would involve more than just injured egos on the floor. "A man who has had intercourse with his wife after having already had one child, or an individual who has had carnal involvement with a woman with children from a previous marriage."

"Huh?" Harry replied.

"Motherfucker," the Professor said firmly, totally in control of himself and the situation. "The strict definition of the term. The way that I am sure that my Negroid friend, Mister Williams, meant it."

"Yeah," Nathan replied, eyes still angrily fixed on Harry's throat. "You're a real politician, Professor."

"You say politician like it's a dirty word, Nathan," the Professor volleyed back. Then, turning to Harry, "What's wrong with politicians? A politician just prevented a fight between you and Mister Motherfucker, which would have ended up with one of you badly injured, and the other most probably in jail."

Nathan backed off. As usual, the Professor was right and, as usual, he didn't pass up the opportunity to gloat over it.

"Politicians are assholes," Harry interjected. His rage now focused on a world bigger than the Last Chance Cafe.

"Politicians are assholes, true enough," the Professor conceded, with a swell of guilt behind his calm, seasoned eyes. "You sound like you've had a bad history with politicians."

"They put good people in jail and let motherfuckers walk."

"So, young man."

"No one calls me 'young man', either."

"I have to call you something."

"Harry, okay? My name is Harry," he said, after a long pause.

"So, Harry. Politicians are assholes. And the people who vote for them?"

"Morons."

"So, Harry, you've affirmed to us that you are not a motherfucker, you hate assholes, and you don't look like a moron. What are you?"

"A human being, okay? Not a neo-hippie, not a Beverly Hills 90210-666 wannabe, not a squeejy hipster living on welfare, not an alternative-grunge-counter fuckin' revolutionary, or any other label you assholes wanna put on me. I'm just trying to make something good happen in a shit world that you assholes and morons let happen. That 'revolution' in the 60s was a scam. The same assholes are in charge. The Illuminati still call the shots. You just made it worse by making them look more 'concerned'. Still one percent on the top, all the rest of us on the bottom. Then they try to sell us friggin' bumper stickers for cars owned by the bank or the repo man. 'Don't ask what your community can do for you, ask what you can do for your fuckinf community.'"

Harry threw two bites of breakfast special down his throat. It would be a long distance between stops. He grabbed the Lysol bottle, the pillowcases he used as a knapsack, and stormed out the door.

"Harry," the Professor interrupted, "it's 'Ask not what your country can do for you, ask what you can do for your country.'"

There was something different about the voice, a different tone, quality, and a haunting source. Like something out of a Twilight Zone movie, for Harry. Complete with the door being closed in front of him by Nathan, punctuated by an ominous look in the black gatekeeper's eyes.

The Professor rose. "It should have been 'Ask not what your country can do for you, ask what you can do for your country, my fellow citizens of the world!!!'" The delivery was that of a seasoned Broadway actor, not a New Mexican expatriate burnout or loser. He continued, "It was an inaugural speech. I was being elected to the office of President of the United States. I couldn't let on that I was being elected President of the Free World."

Harry looked to Nathan for an answer, some explanation... something that made sense of what seemed to be a time warp.

Nathan's reply was more frightening than any Twilight Zone episode. "You say you want to make a difference, Harry. You say you're the last rugged individualist of your generation. Talk to the Professor. The only way out of this place is through him."

Before further explanation could be given with eyes or words, Nathan bolt-locked the front door, pulled the shades down, and put a "Closed" sign in the window.

Harry turned. Nathan set the Professor's table for two. "Professor, two bottles of Coke, tacos, chili sauce, and cigars."

"Cuban cigars, Nathan?"

"From your friend, Professor."

The Professor's face turned solemn as he unwrapped it. "Cuba still makes the best cigars in the world. Fidel has done well for himself and has done a lot of good things in Cuba. Free health care for everyone. One hundred percent literacy rate. Nathan, remember when you had that surgery done? The Cuban doctor was the guy who got you fixed up."

"Yeah, Professor."

"All things considered, I'd give Fidel an A-minus off the record. A pain-in-the-ass, internationally speaking. But at least he still has a laboratory to conduct his revolutionary experiments and I….."

"Professor," Nathan interrupted, "If you sit Harry at this table, promise him what you promised the others, then you do your own cooking, cleaning, and ass-saving."

Nathan was firm. But the Professor had stepped over the line; honor was at stake.

"Harry's hungry, Nathan. I'll talk, he'll listen. Harry can make up his own mind."

A mixture of emotions battled for control of Nathan's mind. The winner was anger. Nathan threw down his apron and grabbed his keys and the gym bag containing all that he considered valuable or necessary.

"Harry, the Nathaniel Williams express leaves one way, for points civilized, in a minute and a half. Fare is a civil tongue and tight lips about anything you saw here. All Aboard."

Nathan left out the back door and revved up a 1979 Buick. The 450,000 mile engine didn't want to turn over, but finally yielded to Nathan's determination.

On the Professor's face, pain. He had burnt Nathan out in all the ways that fire-driven eccentrics and revolutionaries burn out their closest friends and comrades. The Revolution the Professor still fought for was too global, too intense, for most people. And, to the Professor's disappointment, Nathan was one of those people. Or maybe Nathan preferred to live on the world's terms, rather than to die on a suicide mission that the Professor had been talking about, "off the record", for the last four years.

"Sixty seconds... All Aboard!" Nathan screamed out.

The Professor put a quarter in the juke box. Coming over it, "My Way", the Elvis Original.

"It doesn't get played much these days," the Professor commented. "Not too many of us rugged individualists left, right, Harry?"

Harry knew that he had been tested since his arrival and, through no fault or credit, that he had passed with flying colors. He knew that he was being manipulated. He would be a dead man if he stayed, a coward to the cause if he left.

"Forty-five seconds, or it's your funeral, Harry. Last Call." Nathan was the kind of person who kept his word. He never joked about matters of life and death, particularly where innocent bystanders were involved.

"Just one question, Professor," Harry asked.

"My friends call me Jack, Harry."

"Jack," Harry said sarcastically, "what about Dallas? You're supposed to be, like, ya know, dead."

"There was a rumor in 1970 that Paul McCartney was dead."

"Which was true, Wings' sucked."

"Life sucks, Harry. To the unenlightened eye, the rules are fixed."

"No shit, Sherlock. No one's listening. Haven't you heard that?"

"Which is why we have to yell louder!! LOUDER!!!" The Professor's mind tunneled into a volcanic reservoir of molten lava, hot enough to set ten thousand worlds on fire.

"Last Call. All aboard, Harry," Nathan screamed out. "You wanna die young, or grow old? Your call. Ten seconds."

Seeing the Professor drifting off into a world of his own, Harry decided to rejoin the one on the less colorful side of the rainbow. The back door was open, a trap door to reality, pathetic as it was.

"One more question, Harry," The Professor said, by way of a request this time. "All great dramas begin with a coincidence that life contrives."

"What's contrives?"

"'Makes up', Harry. Life makes up only a few accidental meetings. You look like you're one of those accidents."

"Fuck you, 'Jack'. I got a family to try to bring together and a score to settle in the real world. You fight dragons up in the fuckin' sky with some other schmuck."

"I suppose I could get a schmuck to wipe out Carlos Marcello. Harry Diamantis," the Professor said. "Harry, isn't that Greek?"

Harry froze in his hole-ridden runners. He looked at his pillowcases. Like a moron, he had left his surname on the tag.

"My mother was Irish."

"And the Marcello organization isn't dead. Neither is the Illuminati."

"And 'Jack'?"

The Professor smiled. "I believe in a 'what's in it for us' world, Harry. Cooperation is the highest form of self-interest. I see an opportunity for both of us here."

Harry was silent. The Professor knew more than he should have. Or was he bullshitting? The Professor seemed to be a master at bullshit and, for all Harry's tough talk, he was an easy mark for bullshitters. Still, it was a bullshit world, and better to have a great bullshitter on your side than go it alone, maybe.

Nathan's car zoomed off. Harry felt a lump in his throat.

"I'll take that as a yes, Harry?" the Professor asked.

Harry turned around, staring the old man square in the eye. "I know what I want. What the hell do you want?"

"To ask one more question, Harry, for now?"

"What?"

"Lift up your starboard hand."

Harry put on his best poker face and raised his left hand.

The Professor smiled. "Close enough.

CHAPTER 2

"A little-known fact, Harry," the Professor said from behind a pair of half-century-old Navy-issue sunglasses, "New Mexico and Arizona have more inland lakes than any other state in the Union. Another little-known fact is that most of them are connected. The third piece of the puzzle is that the easiest way to Mexico is by water, not land."

The Professor loaded the bulk of the provisions onto the craft. It wasn't a Hyannisport yacht by any stretch of the imagination. In its lifetime, it had been a fisherman's dinghy, an off-season ferry boat, a tourist rent-out, and a transportation vessel for illegal cross-border pharmaceutical and human cargo.

When the Professor acquired it, the heap of wood and metal looked more worthy of being on top of a scrap heap than crystal clear water. But he made sure that the craft was river, if not sea, worthy. The holes in the hull were plugged up, the rudder moved easily and held steady, and the mainsail, which looked more like a quilt, could hold up against even hurricane-force winds. Most importantly, he was sure to give the vessel a proper name.

Few of the locals could put it together, and fewer cared. Why name a boat destined for salvage "PT109?" But it suited the Professor's needs. He was ready for the trip, eager to share the adventure with his new comrade in arms and, hopefully, friend.

As the Professor cast off, he became thirty years younger. Harry felt a generation older, courtesy of the most vicious of the warrior's gods, fear.

"Are you scared, Harry?" the Professor asked, as the boat hooked its hull solidly onto the swelled tributaries of the nameless rivers, which filled each Spring after the snowmelt from the high country.

"No," Harry screamed back. "I just get, ya know, nervous around water. Not scared, just nervous. Hey, you know how to drive this thing?"

"Trust me, Harry. You'll get your sea legs soon enough. Everybody does."

"What if I can't swim? Hypothetically, ya know?"

"Then you'll drown. And the money I promised you on the truck ride out here will have to go to somebody else. Along with the contacts, you need to reconnect with Mickey and Leona, and to settle that legal matter with your father."

"And what's in it for you, Jack?" Harry wanted to know the terms of the deal. He had made the mistake of telling the Professor too much, too early. This New England expatriate may have looked like a New Mexican Santa Claus, but he was just like everyone else. He had to be. He had goals, needs, and "hidden agendas." Harry hated people with hidden agendas. To Harry, a hidden agenda was a lie, a plan that would get him financially screwed, emotionally hurt, or physically killed. What was the Professor's hidden agenda?

As usual, the Professor was ahead of Harry. "Tell me about your family again, Harry."

"Why?"

"Because you care about them. And I can help you."

"Mickey. I miss him the most. A younger brother who was smarter than me. In school, but not in the streets. He stayed at home a lot, read a lot of books. Got himself smart in the head. Then got beaten up when my father started drinking. My Mother said that Mickey needed it. That he had special problems, ya know?"

"I know," the Professor said compassionately. "We'll get him out of the mental hospital."

"And to Montana. They got survivalists up there. Guys who got guns and who don't obey any laws or court orders. And if those doctors think they can keep me from…"

"Leona?" the Professor interjected, trying to keep Harry's mind on solutions, rather than problems.

"West Coast, I think. She liked water, but she liked mountains more. A real animal freak. Went veggie when she was nine years old. I started looking for her in Oregon. I thought I saw her in Portland once, working tricks. She pretended not to know me, kept quiet until I got her up into a room. Turned out it was a guy. A cop in drag. Busted me for solicitation. I'm the one who's underage; he was the pervert jerking off under his panties, and I get arrested. Took me a week to get out; I lost track of Leona. If I find that pervert cop, I'll cut his balls off and…"

"Your father?"

"A dead man."

"You testified against him in court."

"I testified for my mother. If he weren't connected, he wouldn't have walked. I grabbed him on the courtroom steps, just under the statue of that bitch, with her eyes blindfolded closed, holding the scales. If he didn't get what was coming to him inside that courtroom, I was gonna give him what he had coming outside."

"He was a cop?"

"Yeah. When I was a kid, a good one. Solid kinda guy. That's what everyone said, anyway. I believed it too. Maybe it was true."

"How connected is he now?"

"Connected enough to have me running from one end of this country to another. From the cops, the gangs, and the mob. Connected enough to keep my brother doped up on thorazine the rest of his life. Connected enough to keep Leona running away from me, the only one left who really cares about her. And connected enough for me to be on a garbage heap on an inland ocean with Woodstock's answer to Moby Dick!!! Captain Kirk on acid, who measures time with a psychedelic sundial, and pretends he gives a shit about me."

The Professor paused a moment. "So, Harry. You want direct answers. Ask them."

"You know the 'whats', 'Jack'. I wanna know 'when'?"

"When the time is right. You don't know what you are up against, Harry. Even I didn't know what I was up against until it was too late."

Harry looked into the Professor's eyes. Maybe he was JFK, revived with plastic surgery and miracle Hopi Indian medicinals, or maybe he wasn't. But most importantly, this lunatic, who seemed to be able to successfully defy the laws of biology, believed in something. If the Professor believed that he had Presidential instincts, abilities, and power, maybe he did. Still, Harry had to look after his own non-hidden agenda.

"When??" Harry would not take double-talk or fraternal compassion as a substitute anymore.

The Professor hesitated. "If you escalate too quickly and too impulsively, you mess yourself up. It happened that way in Vietnam. Everyone is using their muscle, not enough people are using their heads. We needed more reliable information. It would have been an effective war against communism, not an ugly one."

"And we're headed to where we can get some information." Harry held the tone of his voice firm, but the contents of his stomach shook, seeking a rapid exit out of his pale mouth. "All that work to get tortillas and condiments gone to waste," Harry thought, as he felt himself pass the halfway highway sign to upchuck city. A look ahead at the widening river and ocean-like swells breaking on the rocks didn't make matters any better.

"Look at the horizon," the Professor said. "A man with your vision shouldn't be looking at the water under your feet. You have the qualifications to be a great leader if you look to the horizon."

"Fuck off, Jack. I'm doing this for my family."

"Then look at the horizon. Look at the...." He flinched, then gritted his teeth. His erect, Herculean body instantly cringed up in a fetal position, as if re-possessed by a demon who wanted to return him to death in reverse, and very painfully.

"What's wrong, Professor? You're back!"

"My pills. In the medicine bag."

"Where the…?" Harry fumbled through books, logs, and assorted navigational gear, interspersed between rusted tools and loose wires.

"The fuckin' medicine bag!!!" the Professor grunted through a gut-wrenching scream.

"This leather thing? With the purple rocks in it?"

"Those are herbs. Throw me the bag. Throw me the…."

This time, Harry's delivery fell short of life's demands.

Back pain of demonic proportions led to paralysis. The Professor's hands gave way. The rudder and mainsail were loose, released to be ruled according to the mandates of the river and the winds. And the Ranson's Canyon bend was no place to trust wind, water, or jagged rock, particularly after the biggest thaw-down from the High Sierras in 71 years.

In one heroic move that Harry never envisioned possible for a mortal like himself, he threw the bag to the Professor, then hoisted his body on the rudder and the mainsail. However, as was always the case for Harry, the more heroic the attempt, the more aid and comfort he gave to the enemy.

The boat stayed upright, then took a sharp turn toward jagged rocks designed to dismember anything made of wood, metal, or bone. No Kamikaze ride could have been better planned. No surprise to someone like Harry, who had been well trained in the life-art of self-sabotage.

"What do I do?" Harry screamed out.

"Mainsail starboard, rudder port!!!" the Professor screamed, a purple Hopi communion wafer in his mouth, eyes squinted in pain, hoping that the medications would get into his blood before the demonic ills infiltrated his brain and spinal cord.

"Huh?" Harry grunted.

"Mainsail left, rudder right."

"Oh," Harry grunted. This wasn't the right time to get left and right mixed up either. But when Harry's dyslexia struck, it struck big.

The river informed him of his mistake, affording him enough time to correct it. But there was a small matter of the laws of physics. Harry gazed down at the crucifix on his neck. "If I'm gonna die, I don't wanna die drowning. Kill me on a rock, okay?" The prayer was delivered to whoever was listening; God, Jesus, Harry's mother, or maybe even the Pagan gods Leona was into.

Whatever or whoever was listening wanted Harry and the Professor alive; the boat nearly capsized as Harry guided it through an underground rock canyon, sharp as coral and twice as invisible. Then, in reward for having accomplished his first nautical accomplishment, another challenge.

No one really knew how "Bethune's Brothel" acquired its name. Some say it was a land speculator who wanted to attract miners, gamblers, and others who saw more vitality in dancehalls than schoolhouses. Others said it was named by a whore offended by one too many lecherous river boatman. From the surface, Bethune's Brothel seemed like the most peaceful stretch of river South of the Platte and North of the Yaqui. In reality, it was a myriad of undercurrents that sucked you in, put you in a spiral, then spit you out, eventually.

"Shit!!!" Harry screamed as the boat took a circular course, as if attached to an underwater whale that would shake it off at a time of its choosing or not at all. "Fuck!" Harry yelled up to the sky, "You really are a sadist. You're gonna make me drown here, with a whacked-out ex-President of the United States. I hope you're fuckin' enjoying this!"

Harry looked down. His trousers were wet, and not by river water. Then the Professor woke up.

"I wasn't scared, Jack," Harry screamed. "Really, I wasn't."

The Professor opened his eyes, looked out at the horizon, at the rudder, barely salvageable, and the sail torn halfway down its middle.

"An engine," Harry said. "This thing has an engine, right?"

One look below revealed the worst. No mechanic born of woman could repair the heap of metallic junk which a half hour ago had passed for an engine. But if there was one thing Harry was good at, it was repairing mechanical things, particularly stolen ones.

"It's an engine. I can fix it, Jack."

Harry jumped out of the boat, grabbing the parts as they floated away.

"Shit! I just remembered, I can't fuckin' swim! I can't fuckin'…"

In front of Harry's face, an oar. Holding it, an arm that seemed bigger than life. "Grab it. I'm not losing 109 or any member of its crew. Not again."

"Let me go. Let me…."

"Grab it, Harry."

"But the boat could…."

"Grab the goddamn oar!"

Harry grabbed the oar. The river countered with another swell, an underwater current leading the boat to a capsized collision, and its crew to a whirlwind that held even the fish hostage for an hour or more. Against all laws of physics, the Professor pulled Harry in, tipped the boat around, and then caught an offshore gust of wind.

"Hold that sail, Harry. We have engines, and we have wind. Fuck what the river wants to do with us. It's been out-voted." With Harry on sail and the Professor rowing like an armada of Vikings, they seized back control, then speed. Then, a well-deserved rest.

"Were you ever scared, Jack?" Harry asked as he tried to piece together the engine that the river had chosen to tear apart. "You were a war hero. Or this person you're supposed to be was a war hero."

"Courage isn't the absence of fear. It's being scared shitless, or pissless, and doing what you have to do, anyway."

"Do you pray when you're scared? Like, are you supposed to?"

"I don't know, Harry."

"Do you believe in God, Jack?"

"I do believe in the potential of the human spirit."

"Is God an asshole, Jack? Or maybe a fuck up? Does he make defective machinery and call it creation? Does he have a sense of humor? For some people, is the world built so that the more you try to do the right thing, the more the worse thing happens?"

"I don't know, Harry." The answer was real, beyond politics, religion, or philosophical mind games. The Professor really wanted to give Harry an answer that was correct, or at least one he could use. He had asked himself such questions for the last 30 years.

Harry had done some reading about JFK as a punishment project in school. A forty-page report on Kennedy, or two weeks' detention. It was easier to do the report, particularly with Lori Rosselli unofficially volunteering her services as sole researcher, writer, and editor.

The deal worked well all around. Lori got the best grass available: pure Maui gold, all leaf, some seeds, no stems. Harry got an A-plus term report that he could use to get himself out of the cooler with the principal or sell to another buyer in a school across town. A change of cover could make it sellable to a cuny history major, fetching a minimum of three hundred bucks.

Harry read the report over once to be sure that he could verify his name as author, then two more times for interest. He also saw Oliver Stone's historical screen account three times. He liked the acting in "JFK," the camera work, and even the music. It was a positively visual experience that sank into his head more than he realized.

The Professor seemed to know a lot about JFK. Some of what he said matched what Harry read, some didn't. All of it sounded authoritative;

the truth, minus the personal bullshit. How could this burnt-out hippie-redneck, who looked like he walked out of a bad "Northern Exposure" episode, know so much? No one was that good a bullshitter.

The big thing that concerned Harry was the face. Harry could never recognize pictures of his grandparents when they were younger. How many times has he embarrassed himself when he looked at his Yaya's marriage picture and said, "Who is that good-looking babe in the wedding dress?" "That was me," she would say, fully aware that Harry was now repulsed by her thin, white hair, hooked nose, and three chins.

What would JFK look like if he had dropped out in 1963? Lived a hard life, or even get some plastic surgery? The Professor had the eyes of a veteran 90's hobo, an outcast in a Yuppoid age. And his facial scars looked too symmetrical. Even his bald spot looked like it was created by the paws of man, not the hands of time.

According to the books, Kennedy was very proud of his hair, combing it constantly in private, and always hatless in public. There was a lot wrong with him medically below the neck - Addison's disease, diagnosed as terminal at least four times in his life, requiring clandestine cortisone injections, as well as a variety of lesser publicized treatments. Intractable back pain and a slipped disk after the original PT109 experience in the South Pacific. The international promoter of physical fitness could barely walk without an intramuscular injection of painkillers every few hours. But on top of JFK's head, through it all, there was always a perfect head of hair.

No mortal could restore the Professor's ten horse capacity engine, but Harry managed to resurrect one and a half of its best steeds. He pondered the raw data in his memory, and in front of his eyes, as the Professor guided the craft down a gentle cross-border water route that welcomed travelers, rather than challenged them.

If the Professor was who he said he was, why the good health? Why the obscurity? And why the self-doubt from the most self-confident President in U.S. history since Teddy Roosevelt? Why did the most "winning" President of all time have that "look" behind every boast or statement of cultural superiority? That look that came with the most feared label to the American Male, "loser." This eccentric New England expatriate was biding the rest of his days for that one big break that would allow him to exit life as a winner, not a failure, not exactly what you would expect for the golden years of a President who miraculously ducked an assassin's bullet, and a press which covered the killing with more fervor than the crucifixion of Christ.

Harry gathered all his intelligence, courage, and compassion, combining them into one elegantly put question. "Jack, are you really, like, dead, or what?"

The Professor smiled. At last, Harry was ready for the first real piece of the puzzle.

"If you have your health, you have everything," the Professor said briskly. "True or false?"

"What am I supposed to say?" Harry's composure was thrown off balance by the Professor's optimism. Another hidden agenda, he thought.

"Tell me the truth, as you see it." The Professor's tone was confident. In control of the psychological chaos around him. The way he liked it.

Harry hesitated. "What was the question?"

"Proposition, Harry. If you have your health, you have everything. True or false?"

"True, I guess."

"You guess, or you know? Have the courage of your convictions."

"Okay," Harry spat back. "True. If you have your health, you have everything."

"Good answer, Harry."

"Thank you, Jack," Harry volleyed back, his confidence renewed.

"But wrong. Try again, Harry. If you have your health, you have everything. True or false?"

"Okay. False."

"Wrong again, Harry."

"Huh?"

"The correct answer is neither true nor false. It's 'bullshit'. If you have your health, you have the potential for everything."

"I don't get it, Jack."

"You have to frame the questions and choices people give you on your terms, not theirs. There are lots of bullshit propositions out there that make you pick between black and white, in a world filled with shades of gray." The explanation was sincere and delivered with an open ear.

"Huh?" was the response.

The Professor took a deep breath to regroup his thoughts and strategy. Maybe Harry really was as dumb as he appeared to be. It would not be the first time the Professor had overestimated someone's intelligence or sincerity. Other young Turks he recruited into his private Revolution had failed the test. Why should Harry be any different?

"It's like this, Harry. If you have your health, you have the potential for everything. A sine quo non."

"A what?"

"A precondition that is necessary, but not sufficient. I guess you don't speak Latin." A tinge of arrogance slipped out within the disappointment.

"And I guess you're really into mind games, 'Professor'. As long as it's out here. In your world. Let me ask you some questions about my world. The place where everyone else lives."

Harry struck a nerve, yet again. It was his talent, and curse, a gift he didn't know he had, but which cost him lots of casual friends.

"Ask away," the Professor said fearfully, with a poker face obvious enough for even Harry to see through.

"We'll start easy. Who's Chris Carter?"

"Quarterback for the Vikings," the Professor replied, relieved.

"Wrong!! Producer and head writer for the X-Files."

"But…."

"What's a hood?"

"A two-bit crook who…."

"A homeboy"

"That must be a…."

"If I 'dis' you, that means?"

"To cut me off. Disinherit."

"Wrong again, Jack. Disrespect. Like you've been disrespecting me since I got here."

"I didn't know that I…."

"Guess you don't talk the language of your own people anymore, Mister President."

The dig hit deep and hard. True, the Professor set himself up for attack, but for Harry to get to the truth of the matter so quickly? Even this out-of-the-loop kid knew that Jack was so out of touch with the world that he was once so connected to.

The next test was set up by life. Harry was never a guy who hit you when you were down. Maybe that was why he lost so many fights. The Professor, JFK, or whoever he was, didn't like being dis'ed. He wouldn't accept pity, either.

"Okay. Let's talk medical," Harry said. "Addison's disease is supposed to be terminal. Why are you still alive?"

"Alternative medical therapy."

"What? You sent Apache Medicine Men to Harvard? Bought in Chinese docs with acupuncture needles? Surgeons trained in the Siberian

North? Looked in the yellow pages under E.T. medical services, care of the Medical Association Atlantis."

"Something like that, Harry. But you forgot Africa and South America. Lots more is going on down there than anyone realizes. No one can control those continents. Not the Marcello organization. Not even the Illuminati."

"Nathan says that you hang out with the Hopis."

"They share the knowledge. Their blue pebbles work a lot better than the white pills I used to get."

"And the back pain. Slipped disks. Got your spinal cord rewired at a repair shop teepee in Taos?"

"A branch of the University of Mexico. Galvanotropic surgery. They hooked up electrical current implants to my bones and damaged nerves. Put together in a month what was degenerating for 20 years. An operation in 1966. Highly experimental, and not approved by the FDA in Washington."

"What name did you go under? The same patient number referenced back to the Journal of the American Medical Association in the fifties." Harry could barely remember his own phone number, but he did recall that JFK was written up as an experimental patient in a trial with steroid treatment of Addison's disease.

"You do your homework, Harry."

"No. Lori did. I just know where to get good dope for her."

"Huh?" the Professor replied.

"That's my line, Jack. You're a politician. You're not supposed to admit when you don't know something. Remember?"

The Professor smiled. A nonverbal gesture of appreciation, expressed and understood.

But Harry did have one question. "What about Dallas? November, 1963?"

The Professor remained silent, terror in his eyes.

"Come on, Jack. What was it? A graze in the head that you ducked out on? A fake assassination touched up in the TV editing room? A double, shot in your place? What?"

The Professor hesitated then, just before Harry turned off his ears, an answer. "The Presidential chopper left for Dallas that day. Mine went to New Orleans. I woke up three weeks later with a new face, burnt fingerprints, and a surgically altered larynx. A fresh new identity. Patient 45099. John Doe. Bellevue Psychiatric. A voluntary patient was reclassified as involuntary. I did get a chance to see who paid the bill."

"Carlos Marcello." Harry could see it coming. Marcello was as crude as they came, and twice as vicious. He made sure that his organization was tight, ruthless, and effective.

"Marcello, Hoffa, and Ruby had a drink the day after my double was shot, and my life ended. A toast. That's on the record."

"And what's off the record?" The question slipped out. It had to be answered.

"It isn't ended. Not by a long shot, Harry. We're gonna get them all this time. For what they did to me, what they did to you, and what they did to a million other families."

"Who is 'they'?" It was a simple question with a very complicated answer, requiring another layer of trust and commitment.

"If you want out, Harry, I can put you ashore, give you the money and the names you need, and my best wishes." The Professor took the proof for his feelings out of his breast pocket, a pocket notepad, and a two-inch-thick green paperback of Presidential portraits.

Harry contemplated. This was a second chance for an exit from a trip getting more bizarre by the mile. No challenge to his manhood this time. No lost opportunity for a chance to start over with his siblings in Montana, or maybe somewhere else. Mexico didn't seem to be a bad place to set up a new life, as long as he stayed away from the river.

There was every logical reason for Harry to take the money and accept a hearty farewell handshake from this eccentric old man. But he stayed anyway, possessed by something familiar, yet very frightening. The professor pocketed the greenbacks and the notepad, smiled, and then sang a chorus of "My Way" at the top of his parched lungs.

"Strike two," Harry thought in the recesses of his mind, as the waters around him got still and very deep

CHAPTER 3

The floor overlooking the swelled mass of humanity in New York is 80 and above. In Chicago, the cut-off point is 65. In Los Angeles, a tower on the 40th floor would give you a strategic position over the "little people."

David Deitrick had offices on the 85th floors in all three cities, along with well-paid and solidly owned moles on the ground floor. Nothing happened in his cities that he didn't permit, or at least know about.

At 34, David still had the look that made him so popular in his twenties. He started his career at 19 as a male model, fresh off the farm, shuffling his feet, his big brown eyes firmly fixed on the ground. Elena Riesman, a hard-nosed, over-aged agent with more talent than finesse, inspired young Davey to do something with his life besides trying to become the richest pig farmer in Southern Ohio.

Two years of modeling abroad, then a third in a Japanese business college, taught David the ropes. He also still had the look and some technical skill as a freelance photographer, particularly when it came to using female bodies as subjects.

Then there was David's voice. Always smooth, always effective, always "upbeat," always aggressive. A five-minute conversation with David was usually a one-way affair.

If he was going to rob you by kicking ass, you'd hear about the ten-million-dollar deals he had closed in the last two days, his plans for a hundred-million score next week, and his life story, all repeated twice if you were weak or curious enough to linger there for more than five minutes. The 'conversation' would end with a compliment delivered to you. Something you could feel good about for ten seconds, until you realized it was an insult, inserted to remind you that you were a loser.

If David were going to screw you in the back, he'd lick your ass until it turned beet red. Before you realized you'd been butt-kissed, he had you. You couldn't say no to him, even when he told you he had ripped you off. Rich people like to be ripped off, anyway. They could afford to throw away a few thousand or a million on entertainment expenses. Besides, David ripped them off with "style." He was one of them, a "beautiful" person in what the commoners on the streets knew was an ugly age.

How David inherited the remnants of the Marcello organization after the demise of its founder was a series of accidents, known in the industry as "breaks." David never questioned why a male model, who could barely memorize five lines, got cast in six-figure acting roles on the big screen within two months after his arrival in Los Angeles. David's "look" landed him his first big role, a break that convinced him that he was "talented." After being handed his second gig for the same reason, he felt "entitled." A break was a break, and the last thing David cared about was thanking whoever was working behind the scenes on his behalf. By the time he got his tenth seven-figure acting paycheck, he was his own man, or so he believed.

Like all businessmen, David rose at least two hours before the "creative" people in his multi-national entertainment organization. The phone call came into his office at 7:23 A.M., L.A. time.

David had just finished ejecting his love juices into Bambi MacDonald, an up-and-coming starlet who wanted to be a star. Promises were delivered, as long as Bambi could still deliver, and as long as she would not get pregnant or possessive.

"Mister Riess. How are you this morning?" David bellowed into the speaker phone, as he lapped a generous portion of fifty-dollar-an-ounce goose pate on a fifty-cent Kaiser roll. On the tray were the other obligatory items for a farm-boy-made-good breakfast. A stack of flapjacks, three slabs of bacon, jet black coffee, and two fortune cookies containing a powdered picker-upper, guaranteed to give him a pharmacological edge on the big-city competition.

"There are some unanticipated problems in New Mexico," the caller said.

David's smile dissolved. Bambi's entrance into the room, naked from the neck down, did nothing to revive it.

"Go out to the pool, Babe. I'll be with you in an hour."

"Something wrong, Davey?" Her luscious lips crumpled, her green eyes opened wide, real concern, rare in L.A., absent in the rest of David's harem.

Time for another front. Bambi's head was designed to carry a gorgeous mane of blond hair, not for thinking. "I'll be with you in an hour," David delivered through his trademark "life's great" smile. "And remember, we have that one o'clock at MGM with the director. Be sure you have your lines memorized. You want to be sure he likes you before I tell him he has to, okay?"

"Okay," Bambi replied, almost picking up on the terms of the casting deal, but missing it, yet again.

David instructed his secretary to take the day off, closed the door behind him, and changed phones.

"Give me the details," David said.

"He's gone. I don't know where," The caller's voice dropped to a very sombre low octave.

"Nathan Williams? The black gentleman?"

"The spook sidekick left town. He went East this time."

"The Professor?"

"South, I think."

"And, 'Mister Smith,' is he alone this time?"

"No, 'Mister Jones.' He's with some kid. A nobody as far as I can tell."

From David, hesitation, then a click on both receivers.

"Mr. Jones, how should I…."

"We'll handle this deal the usual way."

"Any modifications to the script this time?"

"Let's go with a larger cast this time," David replied, after another hesitation. "A 'good-fella's' tone. Buddy-picture adventure genre. Comedic overtones, tragic subtext. Lots of blacks, browns, and grays. Surprise ending. You know what I like, but I want to be surprised. You can cast the director this time, but check in with the main office on all creative decisions. We both have to keep our investors happy."

"Of course, Mr. Jones."

"And one more thing, Mr. Smith."

"Yes, Mr. Jones?"

"You have yourself a good day."

"You too, Mr. Jones."

David hung up first, a habit he always kept in business calls. He would have to make another call by eight. This would be Riess's last gig, even if he did succeed.

But everything was still on schedule. The sun rose at 7:43 sharp. The newspapers arrived in the mail slot at 7:50, and the little people down below still barely knew that David was staring down at them.

CHAPTER 4

The inland Sonoran river deltas looked more like a giant pristine lake. Very still, but also very deep and dark. Get lost in them, and you would vanish forever without a trace, like the Professor's eyes and the life he kept telling half-truths about.

"Where are we going?" Harry asked.

"Listen to the music," the Professor replied, singing along to the show tune on the eight-track. "Camelot. Where once it never rained 'til after sundown. By eight in the morning, the fog had disappeared. And there's a legal limit to the snow here in Camelot!"

The Professor looked Harry's way, inviting him to sing along. He returned an over-exaggerated "all okay" smile.

From Harry's perspective, it all looked like "Apocalypse Now-Part 3 1/2". He was Martin Sheen, on some kind of mission to save the world. At the helm of the boat, a divinely-inspired Captain who got his pilot's license from the Ozian Academy of Astral Projection. And up the river, who knew? Oliver Stone starring as the elusive Colonel Kurtz, the master guru who had the answer to the world's problems, Jack's Karmic dilemma, and maybe his own multi-factorial life "situation."

From the Professor's perspective, it was just another bi-monthly milk run, bringing supplies to a "secret political experiment" he called "Camelot Five." Harry had to ask the question.

"What happened to Camelots One through Four?"

From the Professor, silence. Severe depression. Then remorse. Then anger. Then determination, the suicidal kind that got things done, but also got people killed. Harry dared not do anything else except listen very hard.

"What's the most important thing in life, Harry?"

"Strong beer? Good dope? A bitchin' screw?"

"Really, Harry. What matters most to you?"

"Friends. Family, I guess."

"And on a more global perspective?"

"You got good booze, dope, women, friends, and family, you don't need a global perspective." Harry smelled another missing piece of the puzzle surfacing and decided to go fishing. "Maybe a dog? A horse, if you're a cowboy?"

"Harry, you want more from life than taking care of your own."

The Professor was right. Underneath all the tough "I take care of my own and screw everyone else," there was some other agenda in Harry's life, one that even he wasn't aware of himself.

"We're all going to die, Harry. What do you want to experience or do before you die? One thing." The Professor waited.

"To make a difference," Harry confessed, after diving deep into his naked soul. "Ya know. Leave something behind. Women leave kids behind. Sometimes, if we stick around long enough after the boink, we can have a piece of that. I guess I wanna make a difference."

"On one person, one family, or one community, I suppose?" the Professor asked condescendingly.

"No way!!! I'm not a loser. Once I take care of my brother, sister, and old man, no one on the planet is gonna say that I passed through here like a passenger. Everyone's gonna know that Harry Diamantis came to town and left his mark!!! I'm no loser!!! I think big, I'm just, ya know."

"Held back by the Beautiful People? The assholes with the power, the money, the 'style'?"

"The 'code'. They change the rules of the 'code' every time I figure them out. Like a drunk who's holding all the cards and won't let you out of the game. I'll play those assholes anytime, anywhere. And….."

Harry stopped himself. Were all the words he was saying true? Was he really one of those fanatics who would die for the Revolution, whatever it was? He hadn't even lived to see his twentieth birthday, and he was talking like a veteran commando on a suicide mission against the biggest Goliaths the Marcello and Illuminati could provide. Maybe getting Mickey and Leona to Montana wasn't about love, but defiance. Or maybe it was about the most powerful motivation to a third-generation Greek-Irish New Yorker, vendetta. Harry clenched his fist, pounded it on a two-by-four, broke it in two, and tossed the splinters into the water.

"Grade A answer," the Professor commented, seeing Harry's thoughtful, silent expression.

"Fuck you, Jack."

"With ten points for extra credit."

"So, you think I'm a winner?" Harry asked, seeking some kind of real answer.

"Only winners sail on the PT109. Losers don't get their sea legs on their first sail, bring engines back to life, or save valuable cargo. My Memoirs."

The Professor tossed Harry a plastic bag. "Open it. An early Christmas present."

Harry felt himself smile. He felt good about himself. He knew that he could be bought off with flattery, but he didn't care. Maybe it was real praise this time. He opened the bag, hoping to find an ace bandage or seasick pills. It was something very different.

"Books, Jack? Your books?" Harry felt touched, then honoured.

"Memoirs, Harry."

"Fiction, Jack. Adventure novels by 'Jack Franklin Klein'. 'JFK' You don't have enough balls to put your own name on your own memoirs, and you give me these morality tests??"

"People are moved by images, not reality. Excite their imaginations and they'll change reality for you. Warn them that the house is on fire, and they'll put out the fire. Of course, you have to sugarcoat the pill first. The naked truth is too much for most people to handle. You have to make the medicine 'palatable'."

"And anonymous, Jack? What is this? 'President Lehman's Express', by Selena Szokovitz. A Bosnian lesbo. Half black, half Jewish. Very politically correct, Jack. Real palatable to the quiche and cappuccino set."

"'Palatable' used to be supermen with solid Scottish Highlander roots, like Ian Fleming. Now it's multiethnic lesbians."

"But historical fiction, Jack? That's, like, a contradiction. A repugnancy."

"When I was a Freshman Congressman, I sent a leather-bound copy of 'Guns of August' to every member of the House and the Senate, a historically based fiction on how WWI started. If people had read it in 1933, Hitler would have gotten into art school instead of choosing a career in politics. Then I distributed copies of 'The Ugly American' to my Congressional colleagues in 1956. An account of fictionalized Vietnam as it was then, predicting what it would become in 1965.

"Yeah. I saw the movie, I think."

"You should have read the book."

"And if the world reads 'President Lehman's Express', it'll, like, prevent global war, pollution, and starvation? Like the 'Ugly American' prevented the war in Vietnam from happening?"

"I'm a better writer now. With a much better view of the experience, from the inside." The words were carefully chosen, from the heart, and final.

Harry read the thinly disguised account. Lehman, son of a rich Irish-Jewish mobster, got elected to the office as the youngest President in U.S. history. His platform was re-evaluation, change, and action. A "just do it" kind of guy, who came on board after a long string of by-the-numbers bureaucrats. A Jewish-Catholic was hard enough for the American public to buy, but an eager non-conformist was too much. Though rich by inheritance, Lehman was a workaholic, never content to let things stay as they were, and never a joiner. He even refused membership in the Free Masons, an organization that claimed most of the signers of the Declaration of Independence, and all but a handful of Presidents since 1776.

An expert in media manipulation, Lehman came into politics by way of his own TV show, a mixture of politics and tongue-in-cheek comedy. It got top ratings, beating out the variety shows, quiz programs, and westerns.

Once in the Oval Office, change was the prime order of the day. Everyone liked it, except those at the top. Countries deemed to have violated human rights were blockaded, strong-armed in the world economic market, or infiltrated with special agents, who unofficially got their job by whatever means required. A new World Health Corps was established, mostly American, with the mandate of providing for the Third World on its own terms. Young recruits joined in droves. An unfit American was an unhip-American. The First Family was the model family. Artists and musicians were held in higher esteem at the White House than Senators or Lobbyists. Enthusiasm reigned in the hearts of the American people. But after the first 90 days in office, so did panic.

Lehman made his mistakes in terms of actions and priorities. The civil rights movement was gaining ground fast, but Lehman moved too slowly. It took his sister, the Attorney General, to remind him that ignoring 15% of the population that was non-Caucasian would cost him a lot more than political embarrassment. Unaccustomed to fighting for human rights at home and dealing with Mississippi rednecks, Lehman came to Congress unprepared. Half of the Republican Party, and the entire KKK, put him on a hit list for wanting to desegregate schools, restaurants, and voter registration exams.

There was the matter of the arms race with the Russians. The Americans lost the first leg of the space race, even though Moscow and Washington ignored the fact that it was the Germans who sent the first rocket into space, way back in 1941, and never officially admitted that both sides used ex-Nazi scientists as their most trusted technical space advisors.

The matter of San Dominica was the one that caused more grief for Lehman than anyone else. President Lehman ruled over the hearts of 200 million Americans and was the hero for a billion souls worldwide. But the affairs of the two million San Dominicans and their bearded revolutionary leader, Juan Chirino, gave Lehman ulcers every night.

Chirino had been a pitcher in the Georgia Bush Leagues, paying his way through community college in North Carolina. After deposing the infamous Rodriguez dynasty, Chirino decided to set his Caribbean island up as a model utopian society. Whether it was called Marxist, Socialist, Capitalist, Pro-American, Anti-American, or Druid didn't matter. Chirino knew what he wanted to do. In the wake of a revolution that everyone wanted, yet he pulled off, he got to call the shots. If anyone was going to be Philosopher-King on San Dominica, it would be Chirino. Not United Fruit, the American Tobacco Company, or the American mob. Chirino put his own people in charge of the tobacco and sugar industries, and converted the Mafia-run Casinos into book stores. He turned the churches into child-care centers, since everyone in San Dominica would get a chance to work. Hospitals would serve those in need, rather than those with cash. The one catch, a Philosopher-King does not have to legally consult anyone before taking action. Chirino was, in some ways, the most powerful man on Earth, a privilege some say he used for good, and some for evil. "President Lehman's Express" allowed for both interpretations.

Political pressure and misinformation from displaced San Dominicans forced Lehman's hand into action. He organized an American-supported invasion of the island, run and conducted by San Dominican counter-revolutionaries. Indecision and pull-back of American support at the last minute spelled disaster for the counter-revolutionary force, and even bigger problems for Lehman. Add to his list of enemies the Pro-Chirino and Anti-Chirino factions.

Yet, Lehman's 34-year-old shoulders kept the world balanced. The more enemies he had, the more effective he was. Nothing stirred his blood more than a good fight, watching chaos around him, which he incited to shake up a stagnant political system, or what he saw as a shackle on the cause of freedom.

Lehman made many blunders, but one terrible mistake. At the prodding of his sister, he waged war on organized crime. His strategy was sound, his legal staff and intelligence informants top rate. But this battle wasn't about a conflict of interests; it was about a conflict of motivations. Lehman wanted to go to his grave a hero, to be glorified in the history books as long as printing presses printed and people believed what they read.

The Roselli Family was in it for money, as much as they could get, and as fast as they could get it. History was something morons read about in school. Politics was a game played by mobsters who were too wimpy to break the law. Lehman had 1.5 million armed soldiers under his direct command and a 3 trillion dollar expense account. But he had forgotten the most important fact of all, that even he was a descendant of peddlers and horse thieves.

The Rosellis organized the assassination. They hired right-wing fanatics, deposed Republicans, disgruntled CIA officials, impatient civil rights activists, pro-Chirino revolutionaries, anti-Chirino counter-revolutionaries, and even a few losers who wanted to make a mark in history anyway they could.

The hit took place in Denver, at the rodeo finals. The Colorado Legislature had voted down a proposal to legalize gambling, the governor having personally refused a generous donation to the Colorado Health Care Fund. Everyone blamed everyone else, but the people in charge knew that everyone was responsible.

"So, what happened next?" Harry asked, squinting at the sun, slowly fading in the Western sky. "My eyes are tired, it's getting dark, and the next chapters look real unreadable. Like they were written by Einstein on acid."

"Roselli got himself elected President. The country got what it deserved," the Professor said bitterly.

"What about Leman?"

"He lived. If you can call it that. For his good intentions and short-sighted mistakes, he was given the worst punishment of all."

"And what the hell would that be?"

"Banishment. The worst punishment in all primitive cultures is to be banished from the tribe. Disallowed entry, even when you can be of use to someone else. To be denied the right to be useful. That's the worst punishment of all, Harry."

"Being retired? At least you don't have to bust your ass working for a living. Ain't that the goal of everyone who's working? To not have to work anymore, Jack? You got your health, a boat, and cash."

"Enough cash to live. No more. No less."

"You don't look hungry."

"I still am hungry, Harry. That's what still keeps me alive. That's why I still need to make a difference."

"So, run for something under a different name. Run for God this time, not just President."

From the Professor, a laugh. It had been a long time since he had a laugh that came from the head and the heart.

"Howard Stern ran for Governor of New York, Jack. Ask him if he wants to trade jobs for a while. You'd get off on having your own radio show. More people listen to radio personalities than politicians, ya know?"

"Especially young ones who don't take any bullshit." The Professor looked Harry's way, throwing him another one of his hidden agenda stares.

"What are you thinking, Jack? You wanna make me God? I'm having a tough enough time being Harry."

"Playing God is easy, Harry. Being God is a challenge."

"Then you do it."

"I can't, Harry."

"You mean you won't!!! You coward!"

"I mean, I can't." A wave of tears flooded down the Professor's face.

Harry could picture the Professor yelling, grunting, sulking, and even masturbating with a Presidential thermos bottle. But crying? This breakdown was no b.s. Harry had, once again, hit him where he lived when he least deserved it.

"Sorry, Jack. I..."

"Get carried away," the Professor interjected, collecting himself. "You're supposed to get carried away with yourself."

"Jack, whatever or whoever you are now, you can make a difference. A real big one. Ya just gotta, like, get in the game. Don't let the assholes bench you. What are the rules of your game?"

"The others I talked to about it got killed."

"What others?"

"Guys who didn't have the balls you have. Or the brains. Or even the 'style'."

"Okay, Jack. Ya got me with flattery. Throw the blood oath on me, already."

The Professor smiled, took a deep breath, then sighed. "What do you know about Guatemala, Harry?"

"A small country next to Mexico?"

"You know or you guess?"

"I know that I'm guessing."

"And you've guessed right."

"Thank you, Jack, I'll take it any way I can get it."

"Not like Carlos Marcello did."

Harry turned around. At last, no hidden agendas or training drill. It really all did start with Marcello.

"It was my brother Bobby's idea to deport Carlos Marcello in '62 on small-fry racketeering and smuggling charges. Some dated back to 1937, I believe. Our father bent the law ten times worse than that every day, before, during, and even after the War. Off the record."

"Yeah, sure." Harry respected family secrets and the importance of maintaining idealistic illusions about heroes who were, in reality, far worse than even "ordinary" people.

"Carlos Marcello built an empire as impressive as any in Washington. I hated the manipulative bastard, but admired him, too. Just like Castro. Off the record."

"Yeah, why?" Harry responded.

"With me, the war with Marcello's organization was duty. For Bobby, it was personal. In his capacity as Attorney General, Bobby pushed, bent, and twisted the law sufficiently to have Marcello legally exiled from a country he had built and, some say, loved. 'An undesirable person to be residing within the United States,' the paper read. Bobby's passion was contagious. With both of us working together, the Mafia would have died a horrible death by 1964."

"In time for the election, Jack?"

"Politics sometimes dictates its own timetables, Harry. You people never understood that."

"What do you mean, 'we people'?"

"Politics was my business. I don't know what makes musicians take dope, get involved with crazy women, or drink themselves to death. But I try to understand their point of view."

"Good save, Jack. But I know you were b-s'ing. I hope you knew you were bullshitting."

The Professor regrouped, assessing his perspectives and real underlying motives. All systems are still operational, for now.

"Hey!" Harry blasted out. "It just hit me! I'm winning an argument with the President of the United States. The President!"

The Professor allowed his star player a moment of glory, then put the team back to work.

"Italy didn't want Marcello back, and neither did Sicily. Away from wife, family, friends, and business associates, he was banished to Guatemala, a guest of the country as long as he could pay his bills, in cash. Marcello was a man without a country. He was not going to be a man without a cause.

"He re-entered the country four months after his deportation, and stood trial in '63. By October, it looked like we could put him and all his cronies away for good. By November, I was put away, for good. Bobby just gave up. The underworld bosses got back their power, and more. Some of them became legitimate, courtesy of the United States Government, and an even more powerful ruling body."

"The Illuminati."

"A-plus answer, Harry."

Harry paused. The next question would have to be phrased right to get a straight answer. It was the way the Professor worked. Giving him a well-constructed and thoroughly investigated question was like a sign of respect, and, like his underworld arch enemies, the Professor needed respect.

"You had to have someone left you could trust, Jack. Why didn't you call up your real friends and have Marcello kicked out of Washington? Exile the asshole to Bora Bora or worse, Secaucus, New Jersey. Smelliest exit of the turnpike. You know how it works, Jack. You know how to get what you want."

"And you know how they get what they want, Harry."

"Extortion. You kick one of their goons in the balls, they shoot your brother, sister, or mother."

"They go after the innocent ones first. They went after Patrick when I was still the President. No one told me why Jackie miscarried. She denied the rumor about being kicked around on one of those nights when she went out alone, and the secret service looked the other way. She told me she was cheating on me. Maybe because everyone told her I was cheating on her."

"Then your brother, Bobby, was killed in 1967?"

"I escaped and tried to resurface in Cleveland. The labor movement needed reforming. I tried to go public."

"John Lennon?"

"I liked his music. Retribution for trying to get my political message into rock lyrics."

"Teddy and Chappaquiddick? How did they do that?"

"Panamanian drugs in Hyannisport pate can make even a Kennedy do pathetically stupid things. The plan was to get Ted embarrassed and his girlfriend dead. Nothing hurts a Kennedy more than guilt. We may be arrogant sons-of-bitches, but we do have a conscience. No matter what people think!!!"

"Touché, Jack. Touché." Harry overstepped the line.

The Professor needed to say more, and did. With words, not tears, this time. "It was a beautifully designed banishment. Disallow me the chance to make a difference, at anything, anywhere, with anyone. Make an eagle sit on the ground and watch everyone else soaring in the sky. Give him good health, filter him enough to live on, so he can watch the world he so much wants to be a part of. Watch, and never be an active part of it again. Not unless…."

"We turn everything around!!!" Harry extended his hand to Jack. "Mister President."

A handshake wouldn't do it. The Professor had to hug Harry. It was something he never did in his Presidential career, not for the cameras, at least.

Harry had not felt enthusiastic for a long time. He welcomed the lightness in his chest, the feeling that his legs and arms stretched around the world, the fire in his eyes which now warmed his heart. Whatever awaited him on the other side of the setting Western sun, it had to be better than anything back East. It would certainly be different.

CHAPTER 5

"Just one question, Jack. Water's flat. But we've been going up into where it snows, and down to where I'm sweating my balls off, for the last five hours, then back up again. What's up with that?"

"It's the way things are here," the Professor replied. "The ways of the mountains. I'm not a naturalist, so I don't really understand it. But you know more about some things if you don't try to understand them."

Maybe it was two days and nights outside the sight of people. The Professor always wanted to take the most scenic route, which usually meant the coldest, hottest, wettest, and most dangerous. Maybe it was something in the drinking water. It tasted different here, like maybe some extraterrestrial scientist was testing some mind-altering substance on earthling humans. Whatever it was, the Professor sounded more like the Dalai Lama, on his way to a Himalayan Nirvana, than an ex-President planning the biggest political comeback in history.

It had been a long time since Harry had had "off" time. Out here, all he had to worry about was the Professor drowning, or a band of Indians with arrows on the shore who wanted his off-orange/brown mane on their lodgepole. Time to relax, kick back, and wait for a new life to happen.

"So, when do we get to Camelot Five, Jack? They got good dope there?"

"If you want it," the Professor replied, hoping it was a joke.

"Guys to shoot the breeze with?"

"The best. They know how to keep a good thing quiet. I'm sure you'll make at least one very, very good friend."

"Just make sure she's from this planet, Jack. Ya know, Earth?"

"Camelot Five is very much about people tied to the Earth." He started to sing.

Harry knew that the rest would be a surprise. And that there was a good reason to go there. The Professor didn't do anything without a reason and some kind of important goal in mind.

Camelot Five was an American expatriate's Paradise. It was a perfect opportunity for the President who had founded the Peace Corps as a means of both spreading American political ideology and maintaining a global-oriented conscience. Only three years ago, the nameless collection of old mining shacks had housed armadillos and ghosts.

The real human refugee population had swelled with the "political unrest" in Southern Mexico, Guatemala, and Honduras. Luckily, people seeking freedom and survival beat out the CIA operatives or dope smugglers who could have used Camelot Five as a base of operations. The Professor wanted to keep it that way.

Citizenship in Camelot required a legitimate history of political oppression or biological need. Egos and previous ethnic grudges were to be left outside the city limits. Indians, Spaniards, Blacks, Marxists, and even Cubans were allowed entry. The Professor ruled with an outstretched hand, rather than an iron one, from a shack built higher than the others. One bed, four windows, and a surveillance system that served tour purposes only, keep the existence of the mountain hide-out secret from all but the most honest outlaws.

With the help of whatever American dollars he could steal, and whatever practical knowledge about biological survival he could contribute, the Professor saw to it that his subjects were well taken care of. Provisions were provided to feed the body, mind, and spirit. Children in Camelot over the age of five could read at a grade 11 level, if they wanted to. Of course, the books were all in Spanish. The industrialized world cared little about Hispanic Renaissance men and women until they spoke English.

The men respected the Professor's abilities. The women knew him for what he was. Some wanted to do more than admire him from a distance. Harry sensed a special feminine involvement from the tone of Jack's singing.

"Ya know, Jack. When you have the hots for a woman, and she wants you too, you sing a lot. And by the look of that third leg you're sprouting under those Dockers, this "Deliverance" revival down the yellow-brick rapids is about something more personal than politics."

"Grade A answer, Harry. Cross-cultural references, juxtaposed. Melodic metaphor. The most reliable sign of intelligence."

"Who is she, Jack?"

"Maria."

"Wife or side-dish?"

"A platonic friend."

"Ya mean ya boink Greek-style?"

"We don't boink at all. And what's Greek-style?"

"If you have to ask, you're not ready for it."

The Professor lowered his head.

"Been a long time out of the saddle, cowboy? Maybe you don't feel like enough of a winner out on the range yet to boink one of the saloon hall babes in town?"

"Life rewards knights, dukes, and princes with love, Harry. Kings get a more global satisfaction."

"So, Jack. You don't mind if I try to get myself a non-platonic relationship with Maria?"

"Fuck you, Harry! Maria's mine… if she wants to be."

"Now you're speaking the language of your people, Mr. President!"

The title fit, even if Harry wasn't really sure about its accuracy.

CHAPTER 6

"His name is Harry," the voice coldly stated over the phone. It was a woman's voice, a man's tone.

"I thought he was a nobody," David said. "I know lots of nobodies named Harry."

"Harry Diamantis."

"So, he's a Greek nobody. The restaurants are full of them."

David continued reading his new script. He was cast as Jesus on Futuristic Earth. Jesus was sent again by the Creator to bring life, joy, and compassion to a metallic world ruled by an elite class of genetically bred supermodels. A one hundred and thirty million dollar budget about the virtues of poverty and humility.

Another reminder brought him back to reality. "Maybe you've heard of Hardball Harry Diamantis?"

"Shit!!!!" David screamed out. "The don of dons?"

"Exactly. Hardball, himself. He's got a ten million dollar contract on his kid's head, a twenty million dollar reward out for Harry Jr.'s testicles."

"You know, you're either the sexiest babe in L.A., or the bitchiest lesbian on the West Coast. Either way, we should do something together," David smirked. More fun and games, he pondered. Maybe even a 'challenge' before he had her beaten senseless.

"How 'bout a castration, movie-boy?"

"Only if you go first, powerbitch."

A momentary silence on the other end. Verbal joust with David.

Round two started with a bang. "Listen up, movie-boy. Illuminati liaisons are…"

"Pleased with my work, so far?" David asked.

"It would be in your best interest, and ours, if your man succeeds. They want Professor Jack as bad as Hardball wants Harry."

"My asshole will do what he's told. If he doesn't, I have a Rolodex full of shitheads who could get it done. With a lot less government involvement than you people use." He turned the script to page 90, Act III. The showdown between the Apostles and the New Age Romans was getting too philosophical. Too stagnant. Too boring. "Tell me something interesting, powerbitch. I've got better things to do than argue about John Fitzgerald Screw-up."

"The screw-up and the 'nobody-kid' slipped past the perimeter. On your shift."

David's mouth dropped.

"But I'm sure your second-string shithead can cover for your first-string asshole. But don't worry, Davey. We never had this conversation. Not unless you give me what I want."

"A piece of my ass, powerbitch?"

"A piece of your action. I want to see what it's like to be the first female Führer. The time that the Illuminati had a woman as chairman of the board. Sig Heil, you pathetic worm."

She hung up first, but David let her, for now. In matters of the bedroom and boardroom, he never lost his head place at the table to anyone.

Getting the Professor's head and Harry's balls would be David's next order of business. It would buy him a weekend of sleazy sex with the powerbitch, solidification of power in the Illuminati, and a controlling interest in the "new Mafia." Most importantly, it would be fun.

CHAPTER 7

PT109 had two features that its original prototype didn't wheels, and a rebuilt moped engine, for portaging between the inland waterways on the New-Old Mexican corridor.

Harry was grateful to do the last legs of the journey on land, but he was not pleased at having to push 109 across the desert. This was courtesy of three nearly flat tires and an engine that barely worked, thanks to the river's revenge, and Nathan's neglecting to do his customary pre-journey tune-up, which had been part of the non-verbal contract that had evolved between him and the Professor. But the Professor did help push, and the engine would kick in, sometimes for a whole thirty seconds. Working against them were the sun, the clock, and the heavy cargo.

"Do we really need to bring all these books, Jack? I'm not talking about the ones you wrote. All these others. This boat looks like a library."

"Knowledge is power, Harry."

"Not out here, Jack."

"Especially out here."

The Professor looked up, still no one in pursuit. The crop duster he had spotted thirty miles back must have been a drug runner sampling recently-scored merchandise, or a weekend pilot trying to score with a female passenger. Operatives working for the Tri-Conglomerate never did flips, near hits against canyon walls, and nose dives, followed by split-second hairpin turns back up to the clouds. The Illuminati, CIA, and Marcello hired twisted people who were straight soldiers, not crooks. Most had families, houses in burb land, and financial dreams that were always a paycheck beyond the mortgage payments.

Being alone for so long had given the Professor a new instinct for people. He could detect human life within a radius of ten miles, a hundred if the wind was right. It was an instinct that loners and desperadoes acquired whether they wanted it or not. That radar never failed the Professor, and his screens registered all clear.

Harry's screens were far more fuzzy. He was now hallucinating five times an hour. Drug-induced out-of-body experiences were nothing new to Harry, but there was at least some kind of lifeline to planet Earth, and a road map. He knew his mind and the dope. He knew what he could handle and had enough temporary "friends" around to look after his body while he checked out of it. But this whole trip was like a tab of mystery acid the size of a waffle. By hooking up with the Professor, he had bitten off more than he could chew. "If I can find my body and mind again, I'll never do dope again. Not even grass," he pledged to any deity who might be listening.

Then, ahead, a shimmering horizon. More rock? Salt flats? Vegas? Certainly nothing human. Maybe an ET launch pad, with, of course, an "X-Files" film crew. Mexico was supposed to be one of those places where ETs like to land, and by now, Harry welcomed any life form that walked on two legs, even if it was green and wanted to use his liver for biochemistry experiments, and display his brain in some museum on Alpha Centauri. It beat being baked by the sun, or maybe going mad like the Professor, the Prez, or whoever the hell he was.

Madness had its benefits. As the elements drained Harry's energy and enthusiasm, they fed the Professor's. Einstein had been transformed into Arnold Schwarzenegger on steroids. Harry thought back to New York, before the big troubles started.

After losing a job, home, and an abusive Yuppoid "provider," Lori Wilson was forced to get a life on her own terms. She got into art. She was the best skull and bone painter South of Times Square, but still one of the poorest.

It was mid-December when Lori turned into Superwoman. Since Thanksgiving, she had gone without sleep, food, and had handled the coldest New York winter in history with just a T-shirt. All you had to do was say a well-meant "hello," and solutions to all your problems gushed out of her mouth. Then, on the verge of what she called a 'great artistic breakthrough', it all came down. Hyper-enlightened rapid speech became an incoherent language that even she didn't understand. Manic became depressive, then disparate, then mad.

The fire between Lori's ears must have burned her to a crisp, maybe because no one wanted to be sparked by it. Lori said that she would die from spontaneous combustion one day, and nearly fulfill her own prophesy. Thanks to the arrival of "professional" friends, her end was a lot more "peaceful." She acquired new clients, who required her to work with finger paint and ink blots. Her new collaborators were the Tin Man, the Lion, Toto, and the Wizard. Those were the lies the doctors at Bellevue told Harry when he tried to visit her.

Was the Professor zooming past the line? The universe never allowed anyone to get too good, too enlightened. Get too strong, insightful, or determined, and the Mafia bosses up in the sky take you out, Harry thought. It happened to Morrison, Hendrix, Lenin, Phil Ochs, and Van Gogh. Would it happen to the Professor? Would it happen to him?

"A few more miles, Jack," the Professor said. "You see that glimmering up ahead?"

"Am I supposed to?" Harry replied, hoping that the mirage was real, or that if he had wandered into the Twilight Zone, he had company.

"Yes, you are supposed to see it, Harry. We're…."

"There?"

"Close. Very close."

Ahead lay water. Nothing more, nothing less. But it was wet, real, and would lead to some destination point with coordinates on planet Earth.

109's land-gear engine turned on for a full three minutes this time. "All aboard, Harry."

Harry lost no time in climbing on. He felt faint, then regained his bearings. Water was ahead, sky above, books by Chaucer, Salinger, and Dr. Seuss all around him. All of it was strange, but real. Thus far, a "psychedelic" experience.

The Professor offered Harry the canteen, the last swig of water. "Are you all right, Harry?"

"You take it, Jack. That water ahead may not be drinkable, or it may not even be water," Harry wanted to say. "You haven't had a drink all day. I have." But Harry drank the whole thing.

A rush of perspective gushed up into Harry's head. Even crazy men get thirsty. The Professor cared about him. He had to. Something else was "real" to hold on to.

The river gave back what the desert almost took away; gentle waters, easy travel, and mechanical luck. The engine found ten more horses in its gears, and the steeds galloped on, full speed ahead. And why not? Ahead lay a sword in a rock, gold lettering in Gaelic, "Turn off "Camelot- Five Miles."

The Professor put on the eight-track. Harry hated show tunes, especially Rogers and Hammerstein. But his head lifted up as the first lyrics on the main theme to "Camelot" bellowed out of the speaker. And it also had something to do with what he saw on the rocks around the bend.

She was a vision of beauty. Long, black hair flowing in the wind, a floor-length skirt cut up to the waist, showing off legs that could only belong to a goddess. Her left arm was outstretched, inviting the wary sailor into tastefully covered breasts you could get lost in for a lifetime.

"That sure as hell ain't Howard Stern doing a Miss Mexico imitation," Harry commented.

"Maria," the Professor said. He was contented, for the first time since the Last Chance Cafe. The feeling was contagious.

"So, Jack. Does she have a sister?"

"Two of them, Harry."

"Twins?"

"Harry, this is Mexico, not Times Square."

"One at a time is okay, too." With the village in sight, Harry's imagination dwelt on love, not lust. It was something he experienced mostly with women he didn't boink. Maybe now, for the first time, he would experience the whole package, as would the Professor.

Even from miles away, Camelot looked like a multicultural Paradise. In the center, a large community hall. On its pillar, showcased at the same level, a Muslim banner, a Catholic Crucifix, a Taoist Yin-Yang symbol, and a Star of David. They were arranged in a circle, with nothing in the middle. Next to it stood an even larger building.

"The hospital and library. We are a multipurpose facility here, Harry. We cure body, mind, and spirit. A year ago, this place belonged to the buzzards and the ghosts. Now it belongs to, freedom."

"Can I make a documentary about it? I won't use real names or anything, but…"

"In time, Harry. Slow, steady, and determined. That's the only way we'll win the final round."

"The final round," words that would have sent shivers down Harry's spine a week ago. Now they invigorated him.

Maybe it was Harry, maybe his own timing, maybe cosmic timing. "I'll pop the question to her this time," the Professor thought. "A wise king should have a queen," he pondered. And Maria fit all the criteria: A-plus grades for the heart, head, and spirit.

"You can tell what a woman can be by her eyes, Harry," the Professor commented as he saw his beloved at the top of Camelot's observation rock. "You can tell what she is by her smile." Maria's was always invitingly wide and infinitely trustworthy. That smile was fixed on her face, with rusted wires that penetrated through her cheeks, tied in a knot around her head. She held her head high, courtesy of a steel beam rammed into her anus and up into her brain.

Harry recognized it from biology class and the streets. She had been pithed, like a frog. The spike was twisted to ensure that she lost all functions below the neck, but maintained enough of them between the ears.

Death by impaling was bad enough, but it was the eyes that told the most horrible tale. She had suffered before the end, experiencing the worst emotions in the lexicon of human experience; fear, regret, and guilt.

A closer look at Camelot Five gave a more globally frightening explanation. The houses were empty, the heads of residents set up like jack-o'-lanterns in the windows. Their eyes were removed, Masonic-like Illuminati brands burned into their foreheads.

Each was set up neatly, no blood stains. No trash. Not even a door latch is broken. The entire kill was clean, very professional. A lose-lose situation all around, except for the vultures, dining on a pile of human flesh piled ten feet high in front of the Professor's cabin.

The note stuck in Maria's mouth explained the 'whys'. "For trying to make a difference. Go back home, Jack. Hot Chocolate and a blanket are waiting for you. You have been benched. Enjoy it."

CHAPTER 8

"Forgive me, Father, for I have sinned." Nathan's voice was an octave lower than usual, and his remorse was twice as deep.

"How long has it been since your last confession?" the Priest replied from behind the Confessional. It was a long day, and his eight-hour ration of compassion had run out three hours into what was now a double shift.

"I have a . . . friend," Nathan said. "And you have to listen, you overpaid son-of-a-bitch."

"You're swearing in God's house, my son."

"I'm being verbally expressive to you, not God. And I'm probably old enough to be your father."

From the other side of the Confessional, silence.

"Father?" Nathan pleaded.

"What do you want to confess, sir?"

Nathan took a deep breath. He remembered that it's how you're supposed to stay calm. Sergeant Ayers screamed it into his head every day of his 12-month tour. If you can find a few seconds of control in the middle of panic, you might be able to take down a few VC before they mow you down. Ayers didn't make it home. Despite his efforts at self-sabotage, Nathan did.

"I have a friend who thinks he used to be JFK. His name is Jack."

"You did something to Jack?"

"I don't know. I'm supposed to take care of him, I think."

"And what did you do to him? Was it a sin of action or a sin of omission?"

"A what?" Nathan screamed.

"If you tell me what you did, God can help you. Or I can." It was an honest answer. It had been a long time since Nathan heard an honest answer from a clergyman. Maybe the "new Catholic Church" was different than the old one he remembered when he told God to piss off a decade ago, just when his luck started to go bad.

"Are you gay, 'Father'?" Nathan asked.

"I am an ordained priest. I'm celibate." The answer sounded honest. At least it was a man, and he sounded straight.

"I'm not Catholic. That's okay?"

"Sure."

On the other side of the curtain, Nathan saw a nun and two men in well-shined black shoes and blue trousers.

"Cops. You got cops in here. This is supposed to be confidential."

"In here, they're people. Just like you and me."

Nathan glanced outside, for a peek, to be sure. True enough, two of East St. Louis's finest knelt at the altar, crossed themselves with Holy Water, and left. One of them looked like he was doing it out of obligation, the other because he meant it.

"Are you hiding from the law, Sir?" The priest held firm.

"From something a lot bigger than the law, my conscience."

"You did something to Jack?"

"I broke a promise. He gave me this box, and I lost it."

"What was in the box?"

"Some directions. Some things I was supposed to do if something happened to him."

"And something happened to him?"

"I promised not to lose the box."

"And where did you lose it?"

"A truck stop outside of Albuquerque. Nympho in a biker black and an SS hat. White chick. Classy broad with an attitude. Been a long time since I made it with a classy broad. I was horny, low on cash, and…."

"You sold her the box?"

"I didn't know it was missing until I hit the Panhandle."

"Who was the woman? Maybe you remember her name, license plate, family background, where she went to school?"

"We compared resumes before we exchanged bodily fluids. How long have you been making love to a mayonnaise jar, Father?"

The Priest paused. "What do you remember about her?"

"Her face. I could remember it anywhere. Five minutes of white pleasure this Nigger will never forget."

"And you think something happened to Jack?"

"I don't know. I got this feelin' that he's lost. I left him alone."

"Then maybe you should go home and wait for him."

"You think so?"

"Yes. Go in peace."

Nathan got up and crossed himself, like he thought he was supposed to. Within five minutes, he was on Route 66, westbound. Within ten, the phones rang in penthouse offices and basements all over the country. Round one and two to the incumbents. The team of underdogs would go down in the third.

CHAPTER 9

Maria's gravestone was simple. A wooden cross to honor her Mexican father, and a feather-laden mantilla to pay tribute to her Apache mother. From the start, she was a hybrid of two warring cultures that somehow found a way to harmonize with each other through her.

Harry did the digging, and the Professor felt the pain. He stood motionless for the entire afternoon, hoping that the Earth would open up under his feet and end it all for him, too. But the only mercy afforded by Nature was the coming of twilight.

"It happened this way to my brother," he said after a long silence. "Bobby was someone that I could trust and even liked to be with. They always find who I trust and enjoy being with."

The Professor looked Harry's way. "Would I be next?" the drifter-turned-caretaker thought. "Am I ready to die for a cause yet? I haven't even found one." Harry had his own agenda, and he couldn't keep it hidden.

"If anyone did this to my family, I'd kill 'em. No matter who they were," Harry found himself saying. "Ya want me to help you kill the bastards who did this, Jack? Family's blood."

"People like us have to care about other people's families first, and then our own."

Harry knew the Professor was lying, and so did the Professor.

"Make you a deal, Harry," he continued. "You help me set this thing right, I'll see that you, your brother Mickey, and your sister Leona get that house on any beach you want. Coconuts and palms in the backyard, too."

"No water, Jack. And no coconut trees. Montana. Gonna grow cattle, horses, wheat, corn, and Port Alberni Alfalfa."

"British Columbia Cannabis."

"You trying to get a new cash crop for the Canadian economy? Get yourself elected President, Premier, or whatever it is that's in charge of Canada?"

"You have a green thumb, Harry?"

"A screwed up head, ya know? Sometimes a tired one. You ever turn on, Jack? Ever been stoned?"

"Not by choice." The Professor recounted.

"Ever been drunk? Gorked out of your mind?"

"A long time ago. Off the record." He walked toward the boat, preparing the sails for a motorless moonlight cruise. His mind shifted gears. He was already a million miles from Camelot Five and Sonora.

"Come on, Jack," Harry pressed on. "You got mega steroid injections for Addison's disease. All kinds of shit got needled into your broken back to keep you from crunching over. Then all that shit they doped you up with in the loony tune factory after your assassination and the plastic surgery. When they did that nerve damage to your left jaw, so your face looks off balance when you show any emotion. Facial palsy on the most eligible married man in the country. Politics is show business for ugly people, but not deformed ones. Not unless it's someplace weird, like Canada. Don't they have a president up there with facial palsy? Maybe it matches his French accent."

The Professor remained silent. Harry had figured out too much, too fast already, he thought. In some ways, Harry was a slow learner. In others, he was learning too fast, and in the Professor's game plan, acquiring too much information too quickly was deadly. Maria's death had proved that.

"Come on, Jack," Harry continued. "All that dope. All that power. All those women coming in and out of the White House. Ever been out of control?"

The Professor delayed, remembering a million stories and sharing none of them, even with his eyes. "I've never been out of control by choice."

"Then by accident?"

"No. By design, Harry. The best way to control the chaos, and still be alive, is to create the chaos."

"Huh?"

"Wrong answer, Harry."

"What are you talking about?"

"A better answer. But another question, Harry. What's smarter, a cow who walks away from a storm, or a buffalo who walks straight into it?"

"Who gives a shit about cows and buffaloes? People are getting killed here, Jack."

"The correct answer is the buffalo. Because the only way to beat a storm is to walk straight into it. Harry, are you a cow or a buffalo?"

"An asshole who isn't crazy. Not like you might be . . . ya know? It's nothing personal, but you've been through a lot of shit and…"

The Professor turned into himself. "My Negroid associate in New Mexico can give you bus fare and accommodations to wherever you want to go, and some extra expense money to spend however you want. You can help yourself, or others, with it." Jack turned angry. It was the kind of anger that kills a man's ability to enjoy life, but keeps him motivated enough to stay alive long enough to extract revenge. "They still let me keep an allowance. Enough to survive on, but not to do anything worth living for. Then, there is option two."

"What? A new car?"

"The eye of the hurricane," the Professor countered. "Center stage in the Super Bowl for it all. We're handicapped by four touchdowns, outnumbered and outgunned."

"And what the hell is your secret weapon?"

"Desperation. We can't afford to lose."

"And we can save the whole free world if we win?"

"Something bigger, Harry. Your family and mine."

CHAPTER 10

After a navigationally uneventful day-long trip upriver and three portages, 109 rested off the shores of the Rio Grande. Harry had never seen this river that had separated the cultures and ways of life for 400 years. Like everything else in the outback of the New West, it was big. But in a somber way, it was disappointing. No landmarks, no arrowheads left behind from Geronimo, no maps to Yankee gold stolen by Frank and Jesse James. Just water, muddy and slow. Scattered garbage. Some aluminum beer cans. Time to rest, rearrange provisions, and organize the final plan.

"Where to now, Jack?" A simple question, Harry thought.

The answer was more direct, and anything but simple.

"Forward," the Professor said. A decision had been incubating behind his eyes, and it was now time to act. "Got a match, Harry?"

"Got a joint, Jack?" Harry pulled out a two-dollar lighter left on a bus-station seat from one of the four-dollar towns in Indiana.

The Professor took the lighter with a quick, grabbing action. Ever since the expedition started, he had always taken what he needed, but never grabbed anything.

"Getting into the American Spirit again, Jack? Like when everyone is being friendly on the bus down from Albany, then when it pulls into the Port Authority in Manhattan, they tense up and grab their suitcases like it's a paranoia festival, even before the doors open. Guess we're going back to Gringo land where…."

"Got everything you need, Harry?"

"I think so, but…"

"Good, so do I."

Within an instant, 109 was in flames. The newspaper scraps and books made a good kindling, and the gasoline can took care of the rest.

"What the hell are you?"

"Moving forward, Harry. Let's go."

Harry had no choice but to follow the beat of a very different drum. What do you say to someone who cuts off his right arm so he can use it as a club? 109 was more than a boat. It was a way of life, now dying a Viking's death, sinking beneath the depths of the muddy, deep red waters that never gave back.

CHAPTER 11

The license plate on the old truck stashed at the El Paso-Juarez border was Massachusetts, 1966. The personalized license plate, freedom. The body of the classic Ford was as old as the sentiment, and just as tested; more rust than metal, more guts than glory.

The way the Professor drove was another matter entirely. He preferred to make his own roads, taking the service routes when possible, making his own path through the desert flats when he could. He got his directions from the sun, not the road signs, and no obstacle under the bald tires would stand in his way of getting to his destination as directly and colorfully as possible.

"I violated the laws of biology by staying alive. I might as well break the laws of physics, too," Jack said by way of explanation, as the truck rocked and rolled over another set of foothills. "Besides, 'there are no rules for the brave ones.' I stole that from 'Jeremiah Johnson'. I can do that, too. No lawyers for the brave ones, either."

Freedom would get the pair to where they were going, or so the Professor claimed. Small details like the exhaust pipe breaking in half near Waco and the suspension surrendering itself to the elements in San Antonio were no hindrance.

The Professor liked to break down in places like San Antonio, the site of the Alamo. That 45-minute skirmish still fueled the imagination and passions of Americans more than any other, despite the fact that few Americans knew very much about the real historical events there. Revisionists were finding more facts by the day. Many of the "heroes" of the Alamo may have been opportunists, in it for the gold stored there. Davy Crockett probably died from a bullet in the back, rather than five Mexican bayonets rammed into his ribcage while holding up the Lone Star flag.

But some facts would never change. There was an invisible line drawn in the sand here. Because of the defiance of 200 men, an army of 10,000 Mexican soldiers was demoralized in the wake of their "victory." Then they were defeated by a few hundred Texans under the command of General Houston, at San Jacinto, in a battle that cost only six Texan lives.

The Alamo historical site was preserved to honor the dead. The repair shops outside town ripped off the living.

"It'll take me two days to get this vehicle working again," the mechanic said. "If you want to shoot it here, I can sell it for parts."

"I want 'Freedom' to be on the road by tonight," the Professor countered. "We have a schedule to keep."

"At the junkyard?" the mechanic retorted.

"New York. Broadway."

"Right," Harry laughed out, surprised and angry. "We're gonna see cats."

"You said you were going to Chicago," the mechanic interjected.

"On the way to New York. Are there any problems with that, Harry?"

"It's just that I have, ya know, 'history' in New York." Harry squeezed out of his quivering lips. "Some people who wouldn't be all that glad to see me. Not alive."

"All the more reason to go," Jack pointed out.

A New Mexican stand-off instantly set itself up. Harry and his family at one end, the Professor, with his secret Kamikaze mission to make the world safe from itself, at the other.

Harry had nowhere else to go, true. And at least the Professor could pay the road trip bills. Maybe the old madman could deliver on his promises to get Harry that Montana Paradise with Mickey and Leona. The Professor did, after all, never seem to run out of money. Supplies never ran out, as if the Professor had secret stash places for whatever he needed, no more and no less. This was supposed to be a cooperative venture, but the Professor called all the shots.

What other surprises did the Professor have up his thirty-year-old sweat-stained shirtsleeves? An encounter with Harry's old street gang? A reunion with his father, Harold Senior? Even when Hardball Harry was an honest cop, he hunted down his prey by linking them up with likable people, who promised them what they really wanted. "Once you got to know the Professor, he was as likable as they got," Harry pondered. The old coot couldn't have promised Harry a better package. A home in Montana for Mickey and Leona, a jail cell for his father, and maybe even a music and publishing contract for him. It was fragrant cheesebait for a very hungry, desperate mouse. Harry knew that the more intricate the maze, the more pain for the mouse at the end of it. It was his old man's trademark, the sharpest knife in your back from your closest friend.

Harry recalled the tales and truths about his father. With prey taken, Detective Sergeant Harold Diamantis was the most skilled interrogator in the precinct. Just put Hardball Harold in with the suspect, keep the lawyer tied up with paperwork or an attractive secretary outside, and within five minutes, you've got a made-to-order confession.

Harold enjoyed his work. A model shoot-first-and-ask-questions-later guy. After he was pulled into Internal Affairs for beating an undercover cop almost senseless, Harold was told to get another line of work.

Ho Ping fled South Korea without a permit, entered the States without consulting U.S. Immigration, and set up shop as the cheapest Korean acupuncturist-herbalist in Chinatown. Harold arrested him as he was coming out of a food store, replacing his powdered milk with a few pounds of cocaine. A deal was struck. Ping and his family got legal citizenship and "special protection" from his enemies in Korea, who had friends in Chinatown. The Master Ninja gave Harold private lessons in Martial Arts and a share in his health food store. The establishment soon expanded into the distribution of very illegal pharmaceutical products.

One day, when Ping's honor student daughter came home strung out, with needle marks up her arm, Ping wanted out. Another arrangement was struck. Ping's body became bird food for the gulls on the East River, and his daughter and wife were enlisted into service for a Saudi businessman that involved work far more degrading than cleaning toilets at the LaGuardia airport hotels.

Hardball Harold kept what he needed; a knowledge of Ninjitsu pressure points to induce excruciating pain without bruises. All he had to do was press his thumb and fingers on the right spots; all the suspect had to do was scream bloody terror in the soundproof room.

Harry Jr. pondered the dilemma. Self-sabotage took many forms for him. One of them was to mistrust friends and overly trust enemies. Harry's mother told him that sympathy was his greatest virtue. His father, before he went bad, warned him that it was his biggest weakness.

The Professor's miracle pills were dwindling fast. He had barely ten days' supply of tablets left. Though Jack complained of having too much good health, those moments only came after he popped a government-issued painkiller or a Hopi herbal leaf. Without those life-saving "placebos," Jack would die fast and painfully, without time or faculty to prepare for death.

The money was running out, too. Way back in New Mexico, the Professor would tell Harry to buy whatever he wanted and let the store clerk keep the change. Now, even Jack was buying stale-dated no-name chips. As the defiant old coot looked at the projected bill to put "Freedom" back on the road, Harry saw the hesitation of a common man who lived check to check.

The mechanic had little sympathy and less patience. "You want 'Freedom' to go back on the road, or into some scrap heap?"

"Pay the man, Harry." His tone was Presidential, the kind used by men too important to carry money, and too farsighted to worry about short-term financial debt. "We will be out of here by tonight. 'Freedom' will take us where we have to go. We'll pay you time and a half. Not a penny more."

The Professor moved aside. Harry paid the mechanic. He sank into being obliging, then subservient, a habit he slipped into when he was on strange ground, dealing with friends or enemies he didn't know. As the most sober member of an alcoholic family, there was no choice. Karmic casting always placed him in the starring role of peacemaker, no matter how hard he tried to act tough.

"We'll give 'Freedom' the sunshine treatment," the mechanic said, eyeing the fifties and hundreds in Harry's sweaty hand.

"You mean put it out back and let the sun shine on it," Harry countered, punctuating his point with a wide "I got you" smile, without a trace of hatred or condescension.

"We'll have you mobile by closing time."

"Five-thirty?"

"Six."

Harry took back the cash, with the exception of a fifty. "Five thirty?" he said, calmly and determined. With that, he moved on. "One lesson finally learned, and applied," he thought to himself. "Mom would be proud of me."

Harry knew that laurels were meant to be left behind, not rested on. Still, he let himself feel accomplished. Far bigger Goliaths would cross his path soon enough.

By high noon, the Professor was hungry again, even though he had just eaten a cheeseburger two hours earlier. "The medication makes me hungry and thirsty, Harry. Cortisone can do that, too," he commented, as he visited the concession stand outside the Alamo for the third time that day.

"Maybe that shit you got in your medicine bag is cortisone, with some powerful acid and heroin, mixed in with some green lawn grass from the pharmaceutical company that makes it? Some Hopi Indian might be having a ten year drunk on the money you paid him."

The Professor looked at the medicine bag with the dwindling supply of pills. "If that's true, then tenacity's been keeping me alive."

"What's tenacity?" Harry asked.

"What you have too much of," the Professor countered.

"Jack, say Marcello and his goons didn't want to kill you. They keep you 'dependent', which is a lot worse. They set you up with an Indian dope dealer, keep you high and well regulated. I bet that every time you run out of pills, you run into another one of those Hopi mystics."

The Professor turned silent. "I did consider that possibility. But the truth of the matter is that I've never felt healthier than after my assassination."

"No shit, 'professor'."

"What do you mean, Harold?"

The Professor ordered a double order of fries, a chili dog, no gravy, and a large Coke. He offered half to Harry, an offer the young rebel violently refused.

"Look, you crazy old man! My name is HARRY, not Harold! My father's name is Harold. He's a damned asshole! I'm just a screw up. You got that straight??"

The Professor saw a world of pain and unspoken history behind Harry's fiery eyes. "I'm sorry, Harry."

"You don't apologize much, Jack."

"Only when I'm wrong, or mistaken."

"Like the Bay of Pigs? When you, or whoever you say you are, sent thousands of Cubans in to fight Castro, then left them on the beach with no air support."

"Yes, Harry."

"And when you started up a war where fifty thousand Americans got killed!!! Because you wanted to defend American freedom in Southeast Asia."

"Yes, Harry, I'm sorry."

"Are you sorry because you were wrong, or mistaken?"

"Sometimes there's not much difference between the two."

"There's always a difference between being wrong and being mistaken."

"You're right, Harry."

"So, Jack. What's so tough about sitting on the bench and watching life?" Harry said as the Professor bit into the chili dog. "These X-files rejects who you say control you give you a healthy body, enough cash to stay alive, and women, if you want them. All you have to do is stop trying to revolutionize the world. Damn it, Jack, no one wants to be revolutionized, anyway. You got the best deal in the world, and you're blowing it. The retirement package of a lifetime. But you still want to make a difference. Why?"

The Professor looked down at the dry desert dust below, then at the big Texan sky above him. "Some people were born to make a difference. I'm one of those people. And so are you, Harry."

"And what if 'our' making a difference gets more people killed, Jack?"

"And what if you don't get your brother out of that mental hospital, or find your sister, or even score with your father, Harry?"

"So, it is a 'what's in it for me' deal."

"Ask not what your fellow revolutionary can do for you, ask what you can do for the revolution."

The Professor tossed his chili dog and fries to the pigeons, and his caution to the wind.

Harry could only wonder where that wind was taking him. It had taken him upward, like a tornado, trapping him up above the clouds. If it stopped or went out of control, it would be a long fall to very hard ground.

CHAPTER 12

"It's a fact of life," David explained to the investment group around the table at Marni's, between the oyster and salad courses. "Eight out of ten movies in this country lose money. One breaks even, and one in ten makes money."

The gray-haired jury was bankers, not entrepreneurs. It was about money for them, not entertainment, and certainly not mass education. If the movie David was pitching to them was about the corruptness of the banking system, and it would make them money, so be it. But there was something about David's pitches that made him sound like the New Messiah, even when the deals smelled like apocalyptic financial disaster.

"Take 'Lawrence of Arabia', for instance. The only movie that starred Peter O'Toole that made money. And Orson Wells died broke, making those wine commercials to pay off his personal debts."

"So, why should we invest our money into this movie of yours?" the head investor asked.

"Because, Mr. Nakamura, this movie will make money. Every movie our company has produced in the last five years has made money within a year after release. You'll double your investment dollars BEFORE it hits the video stores. Anything after that is gravy, gentlemen."

The group looked at each other, doubting the golden egg laid before them. David continued, "Gentlemen, have we ever disappointed you?"

David's real backers never let him down. It was an arrangement that worked very well, all things considered. All information was on a "need to know" basis. The "don't ask, don't tell" mode of operation was engraved between every line of the agreements, and on the Faxes that criss-crossed the continent, and the world, all going through David's office.

"This movie you want to make sounds fun and artistic, but risky. I assume that you are using your usual distribution system," Nakamura asserted. "Do I want to know how you turn a dime into a dollar with a studio that is already in debt?"

"Not if you want to make money, Mr. Nakamura."

David presented Nakamura with a contract, a golden Illuminati seal on the letterhead that contained specks of the element it represented. Nakamura nodded. His assistants smiled. The accountants took care of the rest.

CHAPTER 13

"If you stand still, I won't stick these needles into your legs," the salesman said, with an effeminate lisp. Carlos Giovanni Leonardo III of Philadelphia was proud of his craft, and no garment on any of his customers would leave the store with an off-the-rack fit. It was a matter of honor and store policy for three generations.

"Professor, tell this person of alternative lifestyle to keep his fag hands off my ass," Harry returned. "He moves one inch up my leg again, I'll be sure he gets that sex change operation he's putting in overtime work for."

"Thirty-two wide," Carlos countered. "Will that be cash or charge?"

"Cash. Pay the man, Harry," the Professor said.

"What if I, ya know, don't want to?" Harry shot back. "This hundred bucks could buy me a private dick for my sister, or a hit of coke for an orderly while he looks the other way and I spring my brother, or maybe . . ."

"Harry, you don't know what state your brother and sister are in, and as for getting compensation from your father..."

"So, give me two hundred bucks, Jack."

The Professor cringed. He looked at Leonardo, hoping that the 29-year-old neophyte would not recognize the man who had been his father's best client. "My nephew, Harry, gets a little familiar at times. He forgets that the right word from me could get him everything he wants, and the wrong word could land him in jail. He's already been in for three months in Detroit, ten days for resisting arrest and assault in Memphis. B and E and car thefts in five other states. Then he skipped out of a court date in New York, a very big court date, two days before his birthday, but he might have a life if he listens to his parole officer, and prepares himself to be properly attired for his new job."

"The Professor did his homework," Harry thought. "Maybe I talk in my sleep. Maybe this old redneck acidhead really does have the underworld and overworld connections that I would need to be reunited with Mickey and Leona, and even the score with dear old dad. Or maybe it's all a big setup, with Hardball waiting around the corner with a rope, chain, and fifty lashes on the butt, as a prelude to a very long stay in a very secluded place."

Harry felt "had." The Professor opened up the throttle on the engines, full speed ahead. "We'll be needing the latest line of shoes, shirts, and jackets. What's in this month, Leonardo?"

"Leather and pastels, with lots of turquoise and lavender. Very big on the schmooz circuit these days on Broadway and L.A.," Leonardo said, with a snide smile directed at Harry.

"And can you recommend a coiffeur?" the Professor asked.

"Antone's," Leonardo replied.

"I'm not trusting my head to a fag," Harry countered.

"And I'm not going to, either." The Professor turned to Leonardo, "Are there any women at Antone's?"

"Straight or alternative?" Leonardo said.

"Straight. They're 78% of the television audience," Jack pointed out.

"Straight enough to give you mainstream opinion, if that's what you're after," Leonardo said.

"Straight and mainstream is what we're after. In an alternative way," the Professor replied, feeling very much at home again as the politician who is friends with both sides, while ripping off everyone. He turned to Harry, "You won't recognize yourself by the time I finish with you, on the inside or the outside."

Harry had forgotten what color his hair was before the waves of coloring, recoloring, dying, shaving, and redying. Changing his identity had become a required skill in his game, staying alive in a world where lots of people wanted you dead.

A look in the mirror at Antone's shocked him. There it was: classic lines, natural brown color, eyes that penetrated through clearly from his brain. Despite his ugly view of the world, he did look like one of the beautiful people, in an alternative, hip way, of course.

"What do you think?" Wanda asked, with flaming red hair down to her ass, a body that pumped as you looked at it, and eyes that desperately wanted to please her man. "I didn't do very much. Just colored some, trimmed a little. Put in a few extensions. Your uncle said that . . ."

"What do you think?" Harry interjected, still stunned to see an improved version of Brad Pitt staring back at him from the other side of the mirror.

"I think you look great," Wanda commented, waving her fingers through his hair.

It didn't feel like an act. Harry was not very good at recognizing a con job from people trying to buy him off with flattery. But he had good radar for a woman who was humoring him. Whatever he had inside of him was winner material, he thought. Worthy of a prize, and a person, such as Wanda.

"So, Wanda. You wanna star in my next movie?"

"No, you're going to star in it," the Professor said. He entered, unchanged in appearance and temperament. He nodded, gave Wanda a C-note, and sent her on her way.

"I just noticed. You don't, like, shower much, Jack." Harry said.

"And I don't shine my shoes much these days either," he replied, referring to his beaded moccasins. "It's part of the image you want to project. But don't confuse the image with reality. Lots of people make that mistake. Contrary to the multitude of self-help books out there, you can't turn a piece of crap into a diamond by spraying white paint over it."

"Are you saying I'm a piece of crap, Jack?"

"No. I just don't know what kind of diamond you are yet."

The Professor was putting a lot into Harry. He hadn't taken anyone this far yet, and Harry had not been tested in battle. In the heat of battle, what would happen? Would Harry fall apart? Would he get reckless? Selfish? Or worse, would he betray the Professor? A betrayal would cost Jack a lot more this time than last. A recently married daughter, and a son who had just been voted Bachelor of the Year. Maria was impaled for his bringing literacy to a small Mexican village. What would happen to Caroline, or John Jr., if Harry brought enlightenment, or even compassion, to the political-entertainment arena that now controlled the English-speaking world?

Harry's next comment didn't make the Professor feel any easier about his clandestine decision, "Jack, I know that you have a next step in that invisible black book in your pocket. I got one in mine, too. My brother, Mickey. You can make me a big star, run me for Supreme Court Judge if you want. But he's gonna be, like, my running mate, ya know?"

The Professor contemplated.

"Decide. Yes or no? In or out?" Harry continued.

"I have a timetable, Harry."

"So do I. We take care of Mickey, then North America. Then Leona, then whatever part of the world you want to save from itself."

The Professor thought. It was one of those quiet thoughts a politician has when he hides what he is thinking behind a blank set of eyes. "If anything goes wrong, you're responsible. And I'll see that you and your brother pay for it before any more of my family suffers."

"Wow, Professor Jack, what a bargain. How can I pass up an offer like that?"

"Maybe you should think of the bigger picture," Jack asserted. "You're a lot smarter than you think, and a lot smarter than even I think."

"Smart enough to know that you have to have a plan to find Mickey, or think one up real fast. I'll wait for you at the hotel." With that, Harry left, bringing Wanda out with him.

The Professor looked at himself in the mirror. It had been a long time since he had done so. Time for another makeover, but from the inside this time.

CHAPTER 14

Harry whistled the theme to "Great Escape" as he and the Professor walked up the path to the Tomkins Mental Hospital. License plates on the cars outside read "New Jersey, The Garden State." Harry broke in mid-chorus, "There ain't no gardens in New Jersey! Just plastic plants in the florist shops. You can't grow nothin' in New Jersey. Nothing grows here. No weed. No peyote. No mushrooms…"

"Shhh", the Professor interrupted, "We're supposed to be plumbers, not comedians."

"And you're supposed to be dead."

"I was, when I was in a place like this." Jack stopped himself, though he yearned to relate the full details of his history as a "defective" piece of psychological meat. His eyes revealed a lot more than his words.

Harry had learned to be very good at picking up secrets about the Professor, particularly the ones he guarded most closely. "Weird that you know the complete layout of this place, and you got three exit plans all mapped out, Jack," Harry commented. "And that you have all that fake hair on your face, and wanted me to do all the talking. Maybe you once rented a suite in this hotel?"

The Professor responded the only way he could, by whistling the theme to "Camelot." Harry didn't join in, but he found his feet marching in tune with the beat. He did not like where they were taking him, and the gates closing behind him didn't make things any easier.

"Name?" the guard asked. At fifty, Ed Williams had three chins, a gun strapped to the right side of a regulation-sized pot belly, and a set of keys hanging from the left. All was his private domain. "Name!" he repeated, authoritatively.

"John Smith," Harry replied. He handed over the ID. "We were told there was a plumbing problem here."

Williams retreated to his non-aggressive "I just do this on weekends" home posture. "Haven't been able to get a decent flush for two days with all the shit that comes out of the nutcases here. Where do you want to start?"

"My Uncle Giovanni knows where," Harry said.

"Uncle Giovanni? Mr. Smith?" Williams looked suspicious.

"Italian, on my mother's side, American on my Father's." Harry tried to hide the quiver in his lips with a wide grin. "Uncle John's slow in the head. Not crazy, just slow. But he knows plumbing."

"And I suppose that Uncle John doesn't speak English, either?" William was trained to ask questions, particularly of people who looked too friendly, too confident about life. This pair seemed too content with their lives to be real plumbers. Real working men hated their jobs, and these two clowns seemed to take their work seriously. They were passionate as well, and being passionate about anything, except quitting early and getting home for the boink with the wife and six pack, was crazy in Williams' book.

"We have papers and a work order," Harry said. The papers were from the Marcello Construction Company. The permit was a portfolio of green Presidential portraits. "I heard that you get prisoners on furlough to fix the plumbing here, but..." Williams examined the papers and cash, assessing his timetable.

It happened a lot like that at The Tomkins Institute. Mental health was a matter of security and profit. And besides, whatever the Marcello Construction Company wanted in Hudson County, it got. Sometimes it was about construction, sometimes it was about destruction. Many patients died here from accidental overdoses of psychoactive meds or brain tumors, then disappeared forever. The chief resident put "Abandon all hope, ye who enter here" over the admissions desk, in Latin. Most thought it said "welcome", in medicalese.

Ed gave Harry a good looking over, up and down, inside and outside, then laughed at the comical old man, said to be a sage, in the third-oldest profession known to industrialized man. He unlocked the door and gave the pair badges, three of them.

"In case you lose one. You wouldn't want to get lost, or mistaken for one of the guests at this institution." William liked making people think like he was talking in code. It made him feel important, and being one of the many people on the Marcello Company payroll was the most important thing he had in his life right now.

"So," Harry said as he walked down the hallway, plumbing tools in hand, his heart deep in his quivering throat. "That was easy. What room do we repair the plumbing in, Jack?"

"124," the Professor replied, looking nervously at his watch, then down at the floor, as he recognized two nurses from his previous stay. They were the kindest to him and would probably recognize him most easily, particularly if they got a chance to gaze into his eyes. "124," the Professor repeated, determination emerging through his trembling voice.

The extra plumber outfit in the workcase was tailor-made for Mickey. They got through the checkpoints with no difficulty or delay. With the exception of a few suspicious eyes, nothing had gone wrong. The Professor was a master of strategy, and Harry was an ace bullshitter. But there was still the hard part.

Harry opened the door, not knowing what to expect. The last visit with Mickey left in his mind an indelible image of a blank set of eyes, a drooling mouth, and a lobotomy scar over the forehead. It was presumably "elective," but even Harry knew that "elective" became involuntary in places like this, where normality is narrowly defined by the most lifeless people in society. Entry on a voluntary basis was easy. But if you wanted to leave, you were labeled involuntary. After all, why would a sane person want to leave a mental institution?

Harry had tried to take care of his brother on the outside, but it was tough. Mickey had baseline organic mental illness. The official diagnosis was schizophrenia with manic-depression due to structural and chemical imbalances. Maybe the by-product of genetics, a bad in utero environment, or some secret beatings from Harold Sr. that Mickey never talked about. Mickey needed professional help. The doctors had diagnostic tools, drugs, surgery, round-the-clock nursing care, and psychological counseling. Harry could only offer love.

As they approached room 124, Harry hesitated. It had taken him over a year to find Mickey, and a chance contact with the craziest Sage this side of the Ozian rainbow to formulate some kind of plan for his release. But could he follow through with it?

"Harry," the Professor said, nervously looking at his watch, and carefully eyeing the East Indian shrinks who were so versant in the chemistry of psychoactive drugs, but so ignorant about the importance of human vitality. "We move now, or never."

"Now?" Harry took a deep breath. "Now!"

Harry entered the room slowly, then raised his cap visor. "Mickey?" he said to the crumpled-up figure in front of him. It was folded up in a fetal position, thumb in mouth, begging for a chance to enter the womb again.

"Harry?" Mickey said meekly, his eyes squinting. "Is that you, Harry?"

"Yeah, Mickey. It's Harry. Harry." For the first time in months, Harry had belief in some kind of Supreme Being, some thankfulness for a Justice that kept the universe intact. Invisible tears streamed down his face as he reached out, awaiting the reunion of his brief, yet very long, lifetime. His reward was hardly what he expected.

"Get away from me, Daddy! Don't hit me!!! Don't hit me!!!" Mickey hid in the corner, thrashing away with whatever he could protect himself with.

"Mickey, it's Harry. Your . . ."

"Get away from me! You're a mean Daddy! I hate you! I hate you, I..."

Then, with a catatonic stare, a blank look of nothing in the eyes, Mickey froze. The Professor acted, pulling a small bag out of his crotch.

"Harry, I can give him this pill and these locals. It will knock him out. We can take him to New Mexico. I still have some friends there who can take care of him."

"What, your Hopi Medicine Man? Or that Nigger caretaker of that 'gourmet' restaurant?" Harry was losing control by the second, and each second counted. The minutes inside the medium security psychiatric ward cost a lot, and went very quickly.

"The pills will bring your brother to a world a lot happier than the one he's in now." The Professor spoke with authority, but with accuracy? Even if he was sincere, could the old geezer be trusted? The Professor may have been the ruling Wizard in Oz, but this was Earth, a very hard and unpredictable planet to do time on.

Harry hesitated, then found himself making a decision. From out of his mouth, without an ounce of logical prethought, "Mickey comes with us. Your people take care of him. If anything happens to him, I'll kill you. I swear to God, I'll kill you, goddamn it."

Three plumbers left, on schedule, and drove out of the institute, on schedule. The Professor made Harry drive. "I don't have a license," he told the kid who had been forced to be a man overnight.

Better to concentrate on the road than to look at the blank stare on Mickey's drugged face, wondering if he would ever wake up again. If he didn't, Harry would deliver his word. But there was another hope.

"Leona. My sister," Harry said, as his mind flashed on the thought. "I remind Mickey of the bad times. Leona was gone before it went bad. She knew him when there were good times. If we can find her, she can remind him of the good times. Maybe he can have good times again."

"Eloquently put, Harry," the Professor said. "Very eloquently put."

"You can find her?"

"WE can find her."

"When?"

From the Professor, another delay, then a direction, well thought out, fully analyzed, and firmly delivered. "Turn starboard at the next light, then port. Then full ahead." He closed his eyes and went to sleep. Instructions would follow later, on a need-to-know basis.

CHAPTER 15

Nathan hated the stretch of sunbaked highway between Albuquerque and Flagstaff. All that desert space made him nervous. For all his freedom-loving words, Nathan's spirit soared in claustrophobic urban spaces. All that people-concentration fired his soul. But the Machiavellians in charge wanted him in the open spaces, back at the Last Chance Cafe.

Nathan pondered what awaited him over the Western horizon. He would put on that grease-stained apron yet one more time. The Professor would ask for New England Clam chowder and baked scrod. Nathan would bring him a smart-assed remark, a bowl of microwaved tomato soup, and a tuna sandwich. A tolerable, sometimes enjoyable, bit of heaven, in the middle of a life which seemed like purgatory. The daydream was interrupted before it could turn into a nightmare.

"A backfire," Nathan thought, as he heard a loud bang under the hood.

The engine missed a beat. The oil pressure gauge dropped two notches. Then two cylinders decided to take an early retirement.

"Thunk all you want, you piece of shit. You will find a way to get 25 miles to a gallon at 70 miles per hour, or die trying."

The words didn't comfort the 1975 Buick, and neither did the appearance of three vehicles behind him. They were plain green. One pick-up, and two Ford sedans boasting 351 engines under very suburban hoods.

The complexion of the drivers was very white, sunglasses hiding their eyes. It was not unusual to see generic vehicles and characterless drivers in the Sun Belt. Maybe they were Canadian Snowbird Amway salesmen, trying to escape the drudgery of another forty-below winter in the Saskatchewan Bible Belt. Or maybe not, said the knot developing in Nathan's stomach.

As the simonized Armada slowly gained ground, Nathan's fears were confirmed. Silent sirens swirled, flashing red lights from the lead sedan and the pick-up.

Nathan caught a glimpse of a chopper, "SunBelt Bible Tours." The barrels sticking out of its window were, in all probability, not zoom lenses for wildlife photography.

"If these Crackers want a car chase, this Nigger is gonna give them one. Let's go." Nathan pounded the accelerator. "If I'm gonna get lynched, it's gonna be after my head goes through this windshield, and after I take out one of those redneck shitheads."

It wouldn't be the first redneck roadkill rodeo in Northern New Mexico. The Southwest was a place for fringe groups of all kinds, good and bad. Austin, Texas, had the best blues clubs south of Chicago. Waco, Texas, served as the home base for the David Koresh family barbecue. Why wouldn't the Klan want to set up shop in one of the most sparsely populated areas of the country that they claimed as their own?

Nathan picked up speed. As expected, the fleet kept up with him. One tried to cut him off on the right. The other edged in to his left. Blaring out of the radios, onward Christian Soldiers. Preparing to blast Nathan out of his seat, 30-30 Winchester repeater rifles. Their holders; uniformed cops, very straight, very official.

Then, an explanation over the loudspeaker. "Sir. Please pull over to the side of the road."

Nathan pondered. What would uniformed State Troopers be doing with local yokels? The State Police knew enough not to go on Nigger hunts in uniform, and the Klan was too stupid to think of going after jungle bunny stew in police uniforms.

Nathan considered again. No one had shot him. Maybe they just wanted to talk, especially the passenger in the back seat of the command sedan. He wore an eight-hundred-dollar suit, an evil eye, and a black carnation in his lapel. As it pulled next to Nathan's left, a pickup prevented a getaway on the right.

"What should we do, Mister Diamantis?" the driver asked, the window open.

Nathan didn't have a good memory, but he did have a quick one. "Harry," he said. "The Professor. The bastard really was…."

"Slow down, please," the officer in the pickup repeated, cool and official.

"Screw you, asshole."

Insult was met with reprisal. The gun barrels were lowered, then fired. Nathan ducked, then jammed on the brakes.

The only thing between the crossfire was air. Nathan screeched out a rebel yelp as the sedans and pickups blasted each other off the road.

The chopper was gone. Harold Diamantis was not pleased. Finally, a victory for the little guy, or more accurately, the individualist. "The South will rise again," Nathan yelled to his assailants, saluting them with his third finger. He wished it could have been a moon, but giving them the finger was enough, at least for now.

The Last Chance Cafe was the last place Nathan could go to now. There was no home left for him to go back to. Not unless he made one for himself. And the possibilities for the "wheres" were endless. The "hows" were taken care of, too. The Professor had told Nathan about a place where he stashed some inheritance cash for his Black sidekick, comrade, and confidante.

Nathan never followed up on the treasure hunt. After all, the Professor was all talk. Honest talk, but still talk. But who else could have brought him into a near collision with the infamous Harry Diamantis, the most likely heir to the Marcello Empire? The stories about the Professor's stashes had to be real. Who knows, maybe he really was JFK, too?

Nathan went further on down the road, then took the first left turn. "It's a politically safer direction than right these days," he commented to the Buick. "But you still can't trust even a left turn. You still can't trust."

On the side of the road, a young woman, her car disabled, tail lights smashed out by a skid into the ditch. She wouldn't be able to walk very far in her red stiletto heels, and her thin imitation-Aspen jacket wouldn't hold up to the biting night winds that would overtake the desert within the hour.

Nathan pulled over before she flagged him down or even saw her face. A new life had to start on the right track, and helping a person in distress, no matter how ugly or attractive she might be, was a prerequisite. And, who knew? Maybe she would be the dream goddess who would turn his life around. Maybe the right woman was all Nathan needed to put all the pieces together to get a real life, perhaps even a happy one.

Nathan pulled out his flashlight and a box of tools. "You need some help?"

"Please," she said, shivering.

Nathan gave her his coat, imagining a kind set of eyes behind the large pair of sunglasses on her attractive face. No doubt, they housed the eyes of a beauty.

He opened the hood. "I see the problem. You have a busted fan belt."

"This one?" she said. The voice was familiar.

Nathan felt the barrel of a revolver at the back of his neck. It shook. Whoever was holding it had mixed motives.

Nathan turned around, slowly, every muscle in his body rigidly tensed up and prepared for the worst. His preparation was not in vain.

"Where's the Professor, Niggerman? And Harry?"

It was her, the Nazi-hooker who pleasured him the last time he left the Last Chance Cafe, then stole the Professor's good luck box, probably because she was looking for dope or dope money. This time, she was in disguise as a Mall-Mama. Her eyes were glazed, like she was under someone else's spell. She would carry out her orders to the death, if necessary.

"If I'm gonna die. I wanna know who did it," Nathan said. "I'm funny that way."

"You wanna know my sign?" Her voice wavered between different kinds of insanity. But her finger held firm on the trigger.

"What's your name, bitch? Your real name."

"Leona."

"Leona Diamantis? Harry's sister?"

She hesitated. A car drove up behind Nathan. He turned around and felt the barrel of a Luger ram against the back of his neck. Then, nothing.

CHAPTER 16

Leona clinched her fist like her life depended on it. A hairy hand popped the needle into the vein, like a rattler stinging its prey after a long tease. Then the juice, a mixed-punch cocktail made from blue, red, and brown bottles hijacked from the Upjohn Pharmaceutical delivery trucks. The kind of drugs that no trucker or pharmaceutical company reports missing. The kind of soul-numbing elixirs reserved for people dying of cancer, or things a lot worse.

"Give me more, give me more," Leona pleaded.

"What do you say?" she heard echoing from the backroom-physician's distorted mouth.

"Please, Daddy. Please, Daddy."

Hardball Harold Diamantis smiled, then let rip with another 5 ccs. Three ccs would have done the job well enough, but Leona did her job like a trooper, and Harold was feeling generous.

Leona smiled from behind glossy eyes. Her father had taken her to regions of Oz that she didn't imagine even existed, and there was no way she wanted to go back to Kansas anymore.

For a jock who failed high school chemistry, Harold knew psychoactive drugs better than most psychiatrists. The concoction he devised for his daughter was pure genius. An addictive sigma morphine agonist to maintain a state of euphoria, cocaine to increase arousal levels, ketamine to ensure a dissociative effect so that body and mind existed in different universes, and propanolol to sharpen her ability to concentrate in the world of forms, when called on to do so.

Leona slurred out "Stairway to Heaven," then let her feet dance to the instrumental accompaniment playing in her head. The song usually lasted five minutes. The next ten would be spent fondling "Harold the Magnificent," the next twenty in bed with him, if he was in the mood.

But today it was about business, not pleasure. Nathan kept his mouth shut about everything involving the Professor and Harry Jr. None of the standard interrogation techniques worked. Nathan saw through the good-cop bad-cop game and even turned it around. The local redneck inquisitors had more vicious designs on each other than on the Nigger they were supposed to break down.

The branding iron made Nathan scream, but not talk. As for the threat of physical mutilation, Nathan said that it couldn't make him any uglier than he already was. Even Mister Ping's pain-pressure points were ineffective.

Name, rank, serial number, and a few "eat shit, assholes" were all that Harold could get out of Nathan. "Maybe this dumbshit Nigger doesn't really know anything," Harry thought. Either that, or Nathanial H. Williams was the worst kind of adversary; the legendary, but sometimes real, kind of loser who was stupid enough to sacrifice life for honor, his survival for friendship.

Either way, Harold would not stand for it. Nathan would break down, eventually. Everybody did. But time was running out.

Nathan had grown from an embarrassment to a threat, as had the Professor. Pressure was coming on Harold from above and below. If he didn't find Harry and the Professor fast, it would be his ass on the line. And it was also about something a lot more personal than professional reputation.

"Leona," Harold said, as she sang to the music ringing in her head. "This man knows where Harry is. Your brother. The asshole who killed your mother."

Leona turned around. She believed the stories that Harold told her. How Harry, Jr. butchered his mother, then put the blame on his father. How her brother sold her mother's body parts on the street, then kept the special ones for himself, displaying them proudly on A chain around his neck.

It was a hard story to buy at first, but the only one that made sense. After all, Harold senior was the one who found Leona starving in a small Oregon town, after the commune she joined went broke, then got busted. Harold bailed her out of jail, then saw that she was fed, clothed, and protected. Most importantly, he gave her a job, a purpose.

Hardball Harold never told Leona who he was working for, but Leona was always satisfied with the answer, "Daddy's Company." Leona never heard of the Illuminati and could barely pronounce it. She had heard of Marcello, of course. But even the Marcellos couldn't be as bad as the carny misfits, cult demagogues, and two-dollar junkie-pimps who had been Leona's employers for the last five years.

Life in the stab-and-grab "alternative world" was harder for Leona than she had anticipated. That she survived as a giver in a world full of takers was a miracle, or a curse. Her brother never even sent her a birthday card. True, Leona forgot a few details like giving him a mailing address. But as Leona saw it, if her brother wasn't caring or smart enough to find her, he was useless. And in Leona's world, virtually everything that walked on two legs was useless, including herself.

"Leona," Harold repeated. "The company I work for we work for. They need to find your brother and Professor Jack before they kill any more people. They killed a whole village of people in Mexico. See?"

Harold showed her pictures of Camelot Five. The piles of body parts, the heads in the window, and the special photos of people seconds before death by execution. Superimposed on them, the faces of Harry and Professor Jack.

"Trick photography, babe. Are you blind, girl!!!" Nathan screamed out, his blood-soaked eyelids big as tennis balls.

Leona pondered. Maybe Nathan was right. He was as sex-starved as any other client she met on the road, but he was gentle as he ate the portions of lust offered to him. He was a nibbler, not a gulper. You could say that he was a gentleman, maybe even a lover. Gentlemen and lovers don't lie, Leona remembered.

"Leona. Harry and Professor Jack came by to visit Mickey." Hardball continued. "They kidnapped him. Then took him away." Harold let a blank stare overtake him, then put glycerin in his eyes. Hardball learned the power of tears a long time ago. When a woman cries, a man is obligated to believe her stories about love. When a man cries, no one can help but believe what he has to say about anything. It worked before. But he had to be sure.

He gave Leona his cellular. "Call the hospital. Ask the nurses. They took Mickey yesterday. I don't know where he is. And if I could only stop it, I'd . . ."

Harold put in another drop of glycerin; insurance. He turned his back, then gave Leona a butcher knife. She would know what to do. She learned torture under the best Satanic cultists in the Pacific Northwest. Membership initiation involved torturing animals. Promotion to the priesthood required doing the same for born-again Christian Evangelists, or their children. If anyone could get answers according to the Illuminati's timetable, it was Leona.

"He's lying. You gotta know that. Please!" Nathan's lungs were punctured, his voice box smashed, but he had to get the words out. "I don't know jack shit about where your brother is, where he's going, or what he's thinking."

Leona pulled Nathan's penis, then proceeded to carve her initials in it. The knife moved in tune with the Satanic verse sung with a child-like voice, "Our Father who art in hell."

Nathan's eyes lost their fire. Grunts of defiance became screams of panic.

"I knew it," Harold said to Jake Number 3, the local sheriff, who sold his department to the Illuminati to pay a thousand dollars for the day's medical bill for his dying wife. "Niggers DO think with their dicks.

That's why they call them dickheads. That's funny. I should be a comedian."

Harold liked to laugh at his own jokes and paid those under him according to how well they laughed along. Jake Number 3 was up to his eyeballs in debt, and arguing with the loan officer at the Savings and Loan was no option. Night-long sessions with Dr. Jack Daniels and Professor Johnny Walker Red at the Casino only made things worse. His wife was dead now. But he still had three daughters.

Hardball pressed on. "Where's the Professor? Where's Harry?" Still, Nathan was silent. Even though he had lost one testicle, the other one was about to be cut off. "You got a tongue, Nigger!!!"

The demonic verses that Leona groaned out to break down Nathan began to come back on her. Leona was intelligent enough to hate boredom, but vulnerable enough to be fascinated with evil. She became seduced by her own spell. The red flood oozing out of Nathan's groin looked green to her now. She was on a fun slide into hell. She was gonna have a party of a death-time with this Black buck, all the way down into the demons' pit.

Something happened to Nathan. Life and death had no definition. The pain had made him numb. He started to sing, then laughed. "I took the blows and so it goes, but did it myyyy waayyyy."

"No one laughs at me!!!!" Harold screamed. "One more chance, then I'll cut your tongue out!!!"

Nathan found himself thinking with the clarity of a seasoned general in the heat of battle, on the verge of a victory. He thought, "Maybe there is something I can tell them that they can use. Something about Professor Jack, or Harry, maybe tell them something that I think is blackmail material. Let them think that they got me, and they'll let me live. Maybe tell them I killed Martin Luther King, or shot George Wallace. They probably did those killings, anyway."

But all Nathan could do was laugh. Harold ranted and raved. Leona chanted and carved, helping herself to nibbles of extra rare steak a la

Nate. Jake Number 3 looked for an exit door out of the warehouse, guarded now by Deputies Hank # 2 and Tom # 5.

"What do you want me to do, Daddy?" Leona asked, without breaking rhythm.

"Break him. Make him stop laughing. Make him talk!!!!!!."

"Okay, Daddy," Leona said. The blade slowly levitated in the air. Then came down.

"ONNNNNEEEEE," Leona screamed out, Nathan's testicles and penis in her left hand. She cut, gloated, and drank the gushing red blood that to her mind was green Kool Aid coming out of a large redwood tree.

"TWWWOOOO," she screamed out again, Nathan's tongue in her right hand. The stroke of the knife followed through, and his tongueless mouth screeched out a silent scream.

"And THREEEEEEEE." This time, the blade went up the diaphragm, taking out the heart without cutting a single rib.

"What are you doing!!!," Harold blasted.

"Pleasing Daddy?" Leona said in a three-year-old voice, through the character of her new puppet, "Mister Nate," made from his heart, tongue, and genitalia. "I am Mister Nate. Ask me no questions, and I will tell you no lies. Unless you ask REAL nice."

From outside, sirens.

"Shit!!!," Harold's reply.

"Fire trucks. Answering a call across town," Jake Number 3 noted.

Harold looked at his watch, then at everyone within screaming range. "The operation's already behind schedule, and you screwed it up."

Harold never accepted blame, particularly when things were his fault. Maybe he should have given Leona only 3 ccs of happy juice. Maybe he should have used a different strategy with Nathan, tricked him into being a partner, then made him a slave. Or maybe he should have killed Harry, Jr. on the courtroom steps after the trial, back in Brooklyn. A planted knife, a gun placed into his crazy son's pocket. Harold could have pleaded self-defense and walked away, elevated to a legitimate citizen by becoming another victim.

Leona was in a world of her own.

"I want her out of here. I want her sober. For the next stage of the operation, I need her sober." Harold would not take "we can't" as an answer.

"What is that stage, Mister Diamantis?" Jake Number 3 knew better than to ask that question, but he did anyway.

"Keeping your daughters healthy, Jake Number Three. That's what it's all about!!"

Harold stormed out. Leona gazed up at the ceiling, now stained with blood. "Clouds, purple clouds up in the sky. See them?"

"Let's go this way, Leona. I'll put you up at my place tonight," Jake Number Three said. She swayed, falling into his arms. They were the kind of arms that grew up roping cattle, not drug dealers or pushers.

"What's your name, cowboy?"

"Ross Cuthand."

"Okay, Cowboy Ross Cuthand. You can take me home now." She kissed him, tore open his shirt buttons, and licked his chest.

The conspiracy of silence commenced. Sheriff Cuthand's men would not say a word. What Cuthand did with the boss's daughter behind closed doors was his business. Only one person cared about the boss. If Ross didn't toe the company line, Hardball Harry would have him cut in more pieces than Nathan. Still, Ross had a hidden agenda, one which was swelling up from a part of himself that he thought was dead. He thanked and cursed Nathan for that "gift."

For the first time in a long time, Sheriff Cuthand didn't care what his men, community, or even his daughters would think of him. It was time to get back to the straight and narrow, no matter what the cost to his own life. Maybe a Gary Cooper High Noon Shoot-out, winner takes all. The Marcello Empire and the Illuminati preferred safer odds.

CHAPTER 17

"Damn. I didn't know Broadway was so, ya know, loud." Harry had not been in the Big Apple for two years. Without realizing it, he had gotten used to small towns with smaller egos.

"Freedom" could barely pass a traffic inspection that would certify it for the junkyard. But Professor Jack, as he now called himself, was proud of the rusted Texas license plate and the antiquated parts mounted on bald tires. "Freedom" got them where they were headed, and that was all that mattered. Small things like finding parking, accommodation, or a game plan were secondary.

Professor Jack had to make one stop at Battery Park to visit his favorite lady. "The Statue of Liberty, Harry. Symbol of American freedom, strength, and defiance. These days, they all seem to be the same thing."

"And . . ." Harry countered, while rummaging through a waste can for a hot dog, the pigeons chose to leave for a lower species. In the ecological hierarchy of the city, the middle class was a legend of the past and a wish for the future.

"You want to know what we're gonna do next, Harry. And how we're going to find Leona."

"Yeah. It did cross my mind."

"The Hopis will look after Mickey. You and me, we're gonna look after the world. And as for Leona, I have some leads that might help us."

"Like Uncle Nate?" The remark was sarcastic, yet hopeful.

"He'll have to take care of himself. Wherever he is."

The Professor had a premonition, not something so unusual for a man of his age, experience, and non-connectivity with mainstream.

"What's happened to Nathan, Jack?!!!"

"I called. No one knows where he is. No one in New Mexico. No one in Kansas City. No one in Detroit. Nathan's the kind of person who always lets you know where he is, or where he's going. Or at least he was that kind of person."

"You know something I don't, Jack?"

"I feel something you should never have to." He turned towards Lady Liberty. "I'm sorry, Nathan. I'm sorry."

Harry allowed the Professor space. The tourists were all on board the last boat out to the Lady of Liberty, and the park benches by the harbor lay empty. Even the pigeons seemed to move away to make room for Jack.

"Grief is a personal thing," Harry thought. Besides, the Professor seemed like the kind of man who had to work grief out on his own. The kind who never cried in public, and had to stay in control, in preparation for a final act of defiance against death. Harry knew he would be part of that act and, in a strange way, he welcomed it.

It was a quiet moment for Harry, too. Somber, reflective but all too brief. Strutting in front of him, ghosts from his past, now graduated to full-fledged demons.

The eyes were deep, cold, and familiar. None other than Ray Wu, head of "The Dragon's Revenge," with a brigade of Vietnamese gangsters-in-training that made the Khmer Rouge look like a Boy Scout troop.

It was the kind of interaction that you couldn't escape. The Oriental Guardian Angels-turned terrorists took whatever they wanted, from whoever they wanted. Dis'ing them would cost you a digit. Stealing from them would cost you a hand. Having a relationship with one of their women invited the worst kind of death. Harry flashed back to torturous times, which he now called colorful and sometimes happy.

Harry didn't know that Susan Chi was Ray Wu's Friday and Monday night woman. She seemed like an Oriental chick with a cool headset and a superhot body, somebody you'd want to have a conversation with after a good lay.

Harry was in it for sex, companionship, and maybe even love. But Susan was in it for revenge. She wanted to test Ray, to see just how jealous she could make him. If she was going to be Ray's first-choice bitch, it would be for more than two nights a week. Besides, if Ray got to cheat on her five nights a week, she deserved the same.

All sorts of scenarios ran through Harry's head as he saw the wall of Dragon jackets approach. He lowered his head, pretending to tie his shoe.

"Hey. Got five bucks?" Ray's voice had gotten deeper and raspier over the last two years. His peach-fuzz mustache was now a full-bodied Fu Manchu, larger than on any of his troops.

"I think I got a . . ." Harry grunted, from the back of a throat paralyzed with fear.

"Will this do?" The Professor intervened. He presented Ray with a ten-dollar bill. "Keep the change. Earth's a tough planet to do time on. People from my planet know that all too well."

Ray walked by, satisfied with the transaction. Had the Professor not been as crazy, the slant-eyed Scarface wannabe would have extracted all his cash and his dignity.

"He got a look at me. Straight into my face," Harry said. "And I'm still alive."

"Yes, but you're not Harry anymore."

Harry glanced into a glass frame mounted on a window. The realization hit home. The clothes, the hair, and even the face looked different. Had he changed that much? Had he become something more than a street kid running from the law, the gangs, and himself?

The Professor's radar was in top form. "Next stop, up there." He pointed to the World Trade Center, the top floor. "Time for a new life, Harry. What do you want to call yourself?"

"God?"

"Or maybe Rex? Latin for king."

"I knew that, Jack."

"I know you did, Rex."

CHAPTER 18

Leona woke up with the rising Arizona sun in her face. It was a pristine sunrise, fresh out of a Louis L'Amour novel. Reds, yellows, and blues all melded into each other, with an ever-evolving color that could only be described as perfection. But all Leona's bloodshot eyes could feel was the painful and very cold light of day and morning.

Leona hated mornings, wherever she was, particularly if it started before noon. Sleep afforded a refuge from a world she could never control. One day, she would sleep through the morning, then into the afternoon, then into the next day, until the time of her death. It was a morning that would happen one day. But not today.

She remembered the night before. Something about carving up a life-sized likeness of James Earl Jones, the scolding words of Daddy dearest, and a cowboy with a large mustache and an extra-large white hat. Maybe she died, and God sent her to her own special circle of Hell, a theme chamber for a cowgirl mouseketeer, who would be poked and fingered by Walt Disney and the Seven Dwarfs for all eternity.

The room had a theme; pink, the cheerfully-putrid color which was a "safe" cross between passionate red and purity white. Pink was everywhere. The curtains covered the windows. The awning over the queen-sized bed. The comforter covering Leona's naked body, stained with fresh blood, vomit, and urine. Leona hated all the pink. But not as much as the photos on the wall.

The featured star, Norma Beth. At ten, she was a cowgirl princess riding a two-hundred-dollar plug horse around rodeo barrels with a million-dollar smile. At thirteen, she graduated to cheerleader captain, the most desired virgin in three counties, then the most secretly-experienced a year later. By eighteen, it was graduation with honors, class of '96, with her lord and master by her side, Ross Cuthand.

"Shit," Leona yelled out. "What the hell am I doing in this . ."

The door opened slowly. Leona tried to get out of the window, but it was stuck, maybe locked.

"Daddy?" Leona squeaked out of her quivering mouth. "Daddy, is that you?"

The intruder stopped. Leona breathed a silent sigh of relief. Maybe it was Daddy Dearest, coming to get a morning blow job after a good screw the night before. Harry kept a few promises, but one of them was to make sure that Leona got screwed only by the best. He bought her out of bondage from the Hells Angels and the Outlaws, a purchase which required lots of bucks and even more connections. If anyone was going to give Leona loving, it was going to be Harold.

"Daddy, did I do something wrong?" Leona said to the half-opened door. She cuddled up against the pillow like it was a Teddy bear, her last good buddy. They would share whatever punishment Harold had in mind, Leona thought. Would he take a strap to her ass, or her wrists? A blade to her head or face? Cigarette burns in her most sensitive areas, the ones that didn't show, and the ones that hurt the most?

Whatever she did the previous night it was bad. Maybe it was naughty. She would pay.

The door opened slowly.

"Daddy?" Leona screamed out. Harold made a second promise to Leona, to never come into her room without knocking or announcing himself.

Leona imagined the worst. Was she sold back to the bikers, who considered her less worthy of respect than a dead dog? The pimp from Portland, from whom she accepted a marriage proposal, before she stole his cash and credit cards? A lesbian with a transplanted dick, infected with Herpes or AIDS?

What came into the room was far more frightening. He wore a white Stetson, bandelero spurs, and a solemn stare.

"Good morning, Leona. Sleep well?"

"You tell me, Cowboy Ross!" Leona screamed out.

Sheriff Ross Cuthand couldn't take his eyes off Leona's naked body. It was the kind of body a man would never get tired of looking at, even after two years of marriage to a possessive woman with three bouts of PMS a month.

"Cowboy Ross, was I good or not?" Leona inquired. "Come on, you can tell me. Was it good for you last night?"

Ross looked down, overwhelmed with a wave of guilt and conscience. But which was it? What crimes was he guilty of committing, and which was he guilty of thinking about? He was a thinker, not just a giver or a taker. Leona was not used to thinkers.

"Come on!!," Leona screamed out. "You owe me now, right? Was I good? Was I as good as your daughter? Did I do you as good as she could do you? Or did you?"

Ross kept silent. Leona couldn't read what was behind his eyes. What was he hiding? How much of him did Hardball Harold really own? Leona didn't smell semen on her, the sheets, or the floor. Was Ross too inhibited to come? Or did he jerk off in the room down the hall while she slumbered in dreamland?

"I'm not good enough for you, Cowboy Ross? Is that it, you pervert?" Leona shouted out.

Ross responded with a tense silence, then softly-delivered words, a volcano of rage beneath them. "Breakfast is downstairs. Shower's down the hall. Norma Beth left fresh towels on the rack, clean clothes on the shower handle." Ross clammed up. It would be a long day for everyone.

"What? You don't care about me? You don't want to punish me?" Leona yelled down the hall.

Ross stopped. Doing the honorable thing would cost him. Certainly nothing new. "Hot water runs out in three minutes, sometimes two. Better scrub up fast."

It would take Leona more than three minutes to get clean. A lifetime of hot water wouldn't wash away all the pain. But she would scrub as hard as she could, anyway.

CHAPTER 19

Harry sauntered into the floral-cluttered World Trade Center lobby, decked out in a $2,400 Armani suit and a thirty-two-cent trailer park attitude. He dreamed about conquering the world above the 100th floor, but his eyes were fixed firmly toward the ground.

"What are you looking at?" The Professor asked, in a Salvation Army imitation-chauffeur outfit still smelling of mothballs and cheap booze.

"Feet," Harry replied. "These high roller guys all wear fag shoes. All except the dykes and power bitches. But get one with good legs and a four-inch heel! I could lick up her feet for a day without even thinking about what was between her thighs. Yeah, Jack. You can tell a lot about people when you look at their feet."

"You can also tell a lot about a person by how much he looks at other people's feet, Harry." The Professor was stern, uncompromising, and compassionate. "Try looking up a little higher."

Harry felt his pupils forced upward, then stared straight into the Professor's coral blue eyes. Young Sir Harry felt the weight of the universe pound down on his size 31 1/2 shoulders.

The lesson continued. "What do you see, or feel, Harry?"

"Piss going down these four hundred dollar trousers, Jack? Maybe I should take another piss. It's been ten minutes since I took a leak."

Harry knew that he was about to come face to face, or face to ass, with the board of Freefly Enterprizes, a multinational corporation that answered to no one, other than the head Illuminati jury itself. Maybe Freefly was the Illuminati, the ultimate ruler of the industrialized world since the Middle Ages. The Professor was well-trained in the art of war, particularly when it got personal and professional.

"David Deitrick is the one we want, Harry, or rather Rex. It's never you vs. them. It's always you vs. whoever you're with at the time. Eventually, you get to the head dragon."

"And Davy boy?" Harry interrupted.

"He's been breathing fire for a long time. Go get him, Dragon Slayer." Harry pressed the button. The elevator was still on the 70th floor. Still a full minute to change his mind, and give fear a last chance to get the upper hand.

"What does 'destiny' feel like, Harry?" the Professor asked.

"Alone? Is it supposed to feel 'alone', Jack?"

The Professor smiled. The elevator arrived ten seconds early. Harry had no time to think, just feel. And what he felt was the mighty sword Excalibur, put into his shaking hands by a man who lived in a kingdom that could only be seen by a visionary, or a madman.

When Harry got off the elevator, all he could see was American Express Gold and Pseudovirgin White on 20-foot ceilings. No graffiti, no smell of a rancid toilet bowl down the hall, not even the stench of ammonia, used in so many places to cover up a multitude of smells and odors that reflected life as it really was.

The hall past the glass doors felt like "nothing." No staircase down, no elevator up. A Twilight Zone heaven, hell, or purgatory, from which there was no escape except "forward." Forward led only in one direction.

All ancient roads lead to Rome, all modern highways get you back to New York, and all multinational hallways put you at the doorstep of Firefly Enterprizes. So it seemed, as Harry let his feet do the walking for him.

As predicted, a security guard in a Brooks Brothers blazer gave Harry the once-over, politely asking him his name, quest, and verification of such. A wrong answer would plummet him not only back down to the ground floor, but probably to a basement jail, in a Police Precinct the ACLU would never check up on.

"You are Rex Harrington-Jones?" the black security guard asked in a very white voice. "How are Sharon and Lance doing?"

"Huh?" Harry replied.

"I did some security work for them. Just curious to know if you knew them."

Harry felt cornered and confused. He had been carefully coached in Rex Harrington-Jones' historical profile. He had all the details memorized. Rex's upbringing in Martha's Vineyard, by a mother with Carly Simon's commercial hipness, and a father with William Buckley's staunch conservative values. Rex's bout with hepatitis left him with some memory loss and a self-initiated trip out on the road. Then his return to the fold, through a dead uncle who miraculously rescued him from a family of Black Migrant workers in Alabama.

Rex's surrogate uncle during his disease-induced sabbatical from the mover-and-shaker class was a Blues musician with ten times more talent than B.B. King and, maybe by virtue of that, a name only known to those in the real know. "Catfish Johnson" played under many aliases, but it was always his own music, with a stage presence that made Robin Williams look like an introverted computer nerd. Catfish officially passed on his soul to Rex at the moment of dying.

So the story about the potential heir to half a billion dollars went.

In reality, "Rex" was a secret embarrassment to the Harrington-Jones clan, dead of an overdose of cheap heroin at a trailer park motel in Tampa after boozing it up with a local hooker.

Harry knew more about Rex than he knew about himself, but not enough to answer a simple question by conventional logic.

"Sharon and Lance Harrington-Jones in the Hamptons. How are they?" the guard asked again.

Was it a false lead meant to trap a non-insider? Did this overpaid doorman with a 45 revolver and the unofficial right to use it, really know one of the first families of the liberal-right wing power alliance, which had unofficially taken charge of America once it was realized that the Woodstock Revolution could be profitable, and directed into market-controlled mischief?

Harry let his eyes go and put his mind into a blank stare. Or did his eyes take his mind into that empty, yet potentially universally-connected, headspace?

"Rex? What's Sharon doing these days? And Lance?"

Sharon and Lance weren't part of the dossier the Professor had collected. Was the Professor remiss in providing the right details? The ones that would matter to people in the real world? After all, to the Professor, what passage of Wagner a man liked, or what kind of raw man an emotionally-stagnated debutante fantasized about, was more important than who spent what summers with whom. Time to assess and deliver, a two-and-three-count, bottom of the ninth, in a game that could decide the rest of Harry's life, or maybe even the fate of what was left of the free world.

The guard cleared his throat, moving his hand within a millisecond's grab of his pistol handle. "Sharon and Lance had some very creative business investments going on there for a while. I was just wondering if.."

"Any Harrington-Jones doesn't tell their real business to any outsider." Harry's tone reeked of caste elitism. "And if they were talking to you about private business, they could not have been real Harringtons, or Jones'. You want to know my name? Tell me yours, so I can ruin your career and destroy your life." The words rolled out of Harry's mouth as if guided by an invisible, yet ever-present, Sage.

The guard's eyes turned down, his back acquiring the hunch required for his position. "The committee is waiting for you, Mister Harrington."

Harry had learned the art of the game well. Three more maxims instantly relearned and executed:

"Say what sounds like the truth, but nothing that you can be pinned down on."

"Make them think you know the real game, even if you don't."

"If you don't like the game they're making you play, make them play yours."

There was a fourth maxim Harry missed follow-up. Beating your enemy in this arena was not sufficient. Destroying him was obligatory to survival, kicking him when he was down and out. It was the only way you got respect, from the spectators, judges, your opponent, or even yourself.

The guard picked up the phone, announced Rex's arrival, then waited for a response. Could Harry beat another Royal Flush with a pair of overused deuces? Would he weaken, lower his eyes to the floor, or let them recede back into his mind, now running on empty at the beginning of the race?

"Where's the can?" Harry asked, with Bedford-Styvestant diction and Gross Point attitude.

"Third door to your left, Mister Harrington."

"And the board room?"

"One more flight up. They're expecting you."

One thought went through Harry's mind as he proceeded down the long corridor. "Chickens walk. Eagles fly. And the easiest place to get burned by the sun is above the clouds."

CHAPTER 20

The yolks on the two easy-over eggs looked up from the plate at Leona, like eyes in a mirror. They wouldn't let her go, holding her tongue and brain in suspended animation. No movement, no thought, just assessment. And the deafening sound of silence.

Leona hadn't heard the roar of quiet in a long time. Maybe it had something to do with Ross Cuthand, or the big unframed land around him. He channeled the spirit of the desert to everyone around him, whether they wanted to listen to it or not. It was a blessing and a curse.

"Your father is taking care of some business in Reno. He asked me to take care of you. Give you whatever you need."

"And want, Cowboy Ross?" Leona saw her chance to gain some ground. It was her place to take it. If you want to be respected as a human being, you have to demand that others pray to you as a goddess, the way of Leona's world. "Sheriff Screwhand. You're supposed to give me anything I want."

"Whatever you need. To stay alive. Protected. As comfortable and happy as possible." The words were well chosen, the subtext firm.

Ross knew Leona's game and the ways of the big city, particularly when he was on his own turf. Like the Navajo, Ross saw the idea of land ownership as ridiculous. But he also saw it as necessary. How else could he guarantee that the plow, bulldozer, or oil rig wouldn't invade the 1500 acres of arid range land which had sustained his family for a century and a half? How else to ensure that there would be some scrap of Arizona natural land still left to pass down to daughter Norma Beth, or her grandchildren?

Ross knew that Norma really wanted to move to Phoenix, maybe even Memphis or Nashville. Norma never liked brown that much and preferred country music to the sound of the desert wind. But maybe she would come back to her family roots one day. Or maybe Ross could adopt a son or daughter, who would pass on the invisible Olympic torch that he carried around with him constantly. Maybe Leona would be that daughter. Maybe Leona could learn that there was more water in hard winter sand than on a warm summer beach.

But Leona didn't want to be bargained for, or with. She could see designs and dreams in Ross's eyes. Maybe he didn't screw her body, but he could screw up her mind. She didn't want to be saved, and Ross was born to be a White Knight with no armor.

"What kind of arrangement did you make with my father?" Leona asked.

"That you be safe and as comfortable as possible. The rest is private." Ross paused. "Just like whatever you tell me here is private."

"Did Daddy Dearest say you're allowed to screw me?"

"I can do whatever I have to, to keep you protected and comfortable. As long as you're alive, fed, not physically injured, and reasonably sober when he gets back, he'll be happy."

"What's in it for you? A free poke? A seat in Congress? Dope? More land? The chance to screw a million-dollar racehorse mare up the ass? Why are you doing this?"

"I gave my word. I keep it." Ross ate, chewing his stone-dry bacon. He looked out the window at the land and the animals he loved more than his life. Very costly land that realtors were all too hungry to eat up.

Leona felt something very odd, strange, and threatening, compassion. Underneath all the "what's in it for me" motives Ross could have for babysitting the biggest brat west of the Pecos, for the most powerful mobster south of Chicago, there was compassion. Plain and simple.

The desert wind shifted and blew through the windows, chilling the eggs on the plate, which had already turned ice-cold. Leona found herself confused, bewildered, then somehow connected to someone and something she thought she had lost.

"My brother, Harry. I gotta kill him. He killed my mother. I gotta kill him. That's what I'm supposed to do, right?" Leona knew the official facts, but for the first time, she wasn't sure of the real story.

"That's between you and your father. Private family business." In the "not-so-bad-old days," Ross had been an active accessory to every crime except murder, child abuse, and cruelty to animals to appease Hardball Harold Diamantis. Then, Hardball needed to keep Ross on his payroll. Now, the ex-cop who once ruled half of Brooklyn was one hit away from sitting on the board that called all the shots. Ross recalled things people talked about, things that happened, and things that were inevitable.

Harold had served the Illuminati well when he took on Carlos Marcello's job of keeping the Professor quiet, isolated, and healthy enough to feel useless. Offering Harry Junior and the Professor would earn him enough favor points with the Elite of the elite, with an option of two rewards - an isolated island Paradise of his own for the rest of his natural life, or a seat on the most powerful jury in the world, for as long as he kept his wits about him.

Member six of the Chosen Circle of Twelve, bearer of a Super Bowl ring and three Olympic Gold Medals, acquired A.L.S.. He spent every day watching his body deteriorate while his brain remained alive enough to experience the agony. Member four contracted an even worse disease-conscience. He was scheduled for a long stay in a comfortable institution or, if he so chose, an accidental overdose of psychiatrist-approved sedatives.

Ross pieced together bits about the Illuminati and Harold's connection to it. But finding out too much was very risky business. Doing anything to stop them was deadly. Ross suspected the worst when his deceased wife contracted a highly deadly strain of virulent cancer. Keep his nose clean, and the same wouldn't happen to his daughters, his horses, or any other friend whom he let become family.

"What kind of arrangement do you have with my father?" Leona asked, demanding nothing except the truth as an answer. "And why does he really want me to kill my brother Harry?"

Ross was very stupid and timid in the ways of the heart, but he wasn't a liar. The cowboy's eyes read "hidden agenda." His mouth said nothing.

Leona grabbed Ross, tossing him against the wall with the desperation of a mother demanding to know the whereabouts of her only child. Ross put up no resistance. He welcomed the beating, the bruises, the pain. Partial punishment, delivered for his failure to stem the tide of history with an 1836 Texan saber and a pocketful of ideals.

Leona asked many half-phrased questions, but they all demanded the same answer - the truth. Finally, Ross put up his hand. "Enough. I've had enough."

"Where's Harry? My brother?" Leona asked. It felt good to believe that her weird and crazy brother wasn't a murderer. Maybe it was just a wish, but it felt comfortable and safe. And Daddy Dearest said that she should feel comfortable and safe at Ross's holiday ranch.

"I don't know where Harry is," Ross slurred, out of a mouth bleeding in three places. "I know that he isn't the one you want to kill."

"Then who do we have to kill to make this thing right?" Leona pressed on.

"Ourselves? We have to become the kind of people who have nothing to lose."

"How?"

It was a question Ross had been thinking about for a decade, maybe a lifetime. He grabbed two pairs of reins from the nail over the door.

"We take a long ride on a good horse. It gives perspective. Sanity. Mobility. Can you ride, Leona?"

"Yeah, why not, Cowboy Ross?"

Ross knew that the only stirrups Leona's feet were used to were those in an abortion clinic. But she was willing, and the answers to both their dilemmas would be found in the Big Open, somehow.

CHAPTER 21

It was a basement under a basement, well hidden from the dark office buildings on Wall Street, and well lit. The former bomb shelter was well stocked with mellow whiskey for the chiefs, beer for the Indians, and rot-gut poison for anyone else.

"Screw the masses. I'm a man of the people. What the hell do those motherfuckin' shitheads think I am? How dare they call me a billion-dollar asshole with a thirty-seven-cent vocabulary?" Hardball Diamantis said aloud, after he opened up the platinum-sealed envelope with no return address, except a Masonic Lodge symbol. "If it wasn't for shitheads like me, assholes like them would have to run the streets by themselves. Those assholes don't even know where the streets are, the goddamn shitheads."

The Illuminati's words were final. Harold Diamantis' admission to the board of boards was put back into a holding pattern until "internal matters are more solidified." Hardball knew that another surprise candidate had popped up for the soon-to-be-vacated position on the board. Was it David Deitrick, grabbing more than what was in the original agreement with the Diamantis Empire? Or was it someone else? Someone with more class, nerve, and tenacity than Davy boy, maybe. Maybe "Professor Jack" was in on it. The whole thing had the smell of vendetta, and the Anglo-Irish Professor believed in vendetta as much as any Sicilian Mafioso or West Side Greek diner.

But for the ex-cop from the Brooklyn neighborhood inhabited by more rats than people, who swore he'd never be at the bottom of any totem pole again, it all boiled down to one thing, rejection.

Rejection always got Hardball Harry depressed, and he got rid of depression with anger. The more helpless the victim, the better. Jean-Paul LeBlanc was as good a punching bag as anyone else. He was accessible, and he had extremely valuable information. The kind that could get Harold back on the good side of the Illuminati central committee.

LeBlanc had the good fortune of being promoted from top janitor of the Museum of North American History to reserve tour guide. LeBlanc had been a portrait painter in high school in Montreal, then had to settle for painting shingles in Queens to support an all-too-brief art course at N.Y.U.

LeBlanc studied eyes a lot. One day, he spotted what looked like a badly matched father and son team in the Presidential portrait gallery. Jean-Paul had seen punk street kids decked out in high-roller fashion gear, but he had never seen Presidential eyes in a down-and-out hobo. He snuck in a sketch of the enigma and hung it in the presidential gallery. It was a simple black and white entitled "The Professor."

Jean-Paul hoped to be famous one day. He didn't anticipate having the FBI at his door serving him papers for a court hearing, then ten minutes later being abducted by Hardball Harry's private goon squad.

LeBlanc liked to paint in vivid reds with deep, rich flesh tones. After stage I of the standard Hardball Diamantis interview, Jean-Paul looked like his worst nightmare. Harold put a full-length mirror in front of his blood-soaked eyes.

"Look, Jean-Paul," Harry sneered. "X-ray of an artist. Self-portrait. We can strip your skin off next. Put a crown of thorns on your head, cut off your balls, and make you the first eunuch Jesus. Or, you can tell me where the Professor and the wonder kid went."

"I don't know," Jean-Paul screamed out, in English, French, German, then his own language of silent scream.

Hardball hesitated. "Maybe you don't know, stupid Canuck piece of shit. You know, Montreal's the dumbest city in the world. You let the Hell's Angels own that place. You go to war with the rest of Canada to demand your right to have French only on all the traffic ramps and condom machines. You're a dumbshit piece of shit from a dumbshit city in a dumbshit country. You probably wouldn't recognize your own dick if you saw it. But we can stretch it out for you, so you could suck yourself dry. But for now, we'll just admire how compact it is."

Hardball widened his smile, the signal for the cronies. Sadistic laughter echoed through the smoke-filled room. Jean-Paul breathed a sigh of relief, then whispered a prayer of thanks to a God he had not talked to for years.

Harold let the party go on, then refocused on business. "The hands."

A large man with deep-seated eyes pulled out a razor-sharp machete. In his hands, it could chop down a petrified redwood without leaving a spoonful of sawdust on the ground. Everyone knew him as Bruno, a simple name for a quiet giant, whose main function was to make others feel smaller than shit.

"No!!! Not my hands!" Jean-Paul pleaded. "Better to kill me than to take my hands. I know nothing about the Professor and his companion. Nothing except what you see in the pictures. Better to take my life than my hands!!!"

Jean-Paul could not have been more sincere and honest. Harry acted appropriately.

"Bruno, do the honors." The words were soft, the cuts smooth. A right hand fell to the ground, then the left forelimb just below the elbow. Then the screams.

"Shut this asshole up. He's giving me indigestion and a goddamn headache. I'm not gonna upchuck that rotten shrimp lasagna for this Canuck frog." Hardball had been though a hard day, and just wanted to go home.

Bruno took a final slice, across the neck with a smooth, decisive blow. One more artist's head fell to the Philistines' guillotine. It fell at just the right angle, the eyes facing forward, the base of the neck firmly on the floor. Bruno took a bow. Money exchanged hands.

"Ten in a row. Snake eyes," a lucky winner yelled out of the crowd. Harold picked up the head by its hair. "Yer lucky I ate lasagna today, frogman. The Professor and Harry Junior are gonna die a hell of a lot uglier than you did, pal."

A picture was taken, a collection for the Diamantis memoirs. "Artist with head in hand," Hardball proposed. The rest of the corpse would be used for the usual purposes. Appendages for phony kidnappings. Body organs for sale to Mexican and East Indian transplant physicians. Loose flesh for meat loaf at "Happy Harold's Food Emporium," a chain which had infiltrated every Yuppie neighborhood from Scarsdale to Lido Beach.

CHAPTER 22

Harry washed his hands after treating himself to a piss in the executive level of Firefly Enterprizes. With soap. For a full three minutes. The most he usually did was run his hands under the water. But it felt good having a servant in uniform prepared to hand him a towel before he even asked for it.

But was it service, or surveillance? Maybe this diamond-class shoe-shine man was a spy, measuring a man's ability to get or stay in the Firefly upper echelon by the size of his dick, or how long it took between whipping it out of the zipper and delivering a stream of yellow nectar to appease the porcelain gods. But for Harry, size remained a preoccupation. "Too big and the power bitches feel threatened," Harry thought. "Too small and you get laughed at by the other guys. But big or small, it all depends on how you play it."

"You guys get to watch chicks take a piss and wash themselves?" Harry asked, as he gave himself another visual once-over check before catching on to an open zipper between his legs for a third time. "Maybe there's a peephole through this mirror." Harry put out his hand for the third time. This round, he didn't snatch it back. His reward was a soft towel, the kind you stole from only the best hotels.

The attendant turned his eyes downward. He smiled slightly under his extra-large Latino mustache, then handed Harry a towel, the stone-cold look of solemn officiality on his face.

If there was a peephole through the mirror, it would lead to a place a lot more private than the women's can. Harry decided to go for it.

"Ya know what's missing here? Graffiti. Non-solicited calligraphic art. I bet they got some

real interesting non-solicited calligraphic art in the woman's can.

Harry caught sight of a laugh under the mustache, which was probably grown to display the consigiere's machismo manhood and hide his more vulnerable emotions. It felt good to elicit a positive emotion in somebody, one that gave pleasure without retribution.

Harry's hands were clean and dry, even under the fingernails. Time to get down and fight dirty.

Harry was led down several more corridors by a secretary who looked like she had spent half her life in the Marine Corp, and the other as a two-hundred-dollar-an-hour hooker. But whether she was official or alluring, Veronica Miller had class and a thorough knowledge of the protocol. The protocol this far into the inner chamber was that humor was strictly forbidden.

The paintings on the walls were all originals by Van Gogh, Rembrants, and Picassos. Harry found himself developing an instant appreciation for art, actually believing the complimentary comments about the six-figure masterpieces he spouted off to Veronica.

Then the wing turned religious. Crosses, medieval reliefs, and the ultimately most scary symbol. It looked familiar, inviting, and like a foreshadowing of apocalyptic doom. The most frightening were the Masonic symbols, framed by graphic designs Harry didn't recognize.

It looked like Mormon gone 25th century, with silent E.T. and Atlantian partners, harsh geometric angles with likenesses of the American Founding Fathers, that made them look more like angry gods than visionary men. Prominently featured was the pyramid with the big eye on top, the one on the U.S. one-dollar bill. Harry spent and valued the dollar as much as any other red-blooded American. But he never looked at the eye on top of the pyramid. It always scared him. Every time he looked at it down in the real world, he got the urge to exchange the greenback for goods, or any amount of change he could get. No surprise that this hallway was cluttered with pyramids with eyes on top.

It was the same eye that Harry had seen every day of his life, on every dollar bill he had earned, borrowed, or stolen. The ever-watchful eye, from a place always inaccessible and ever powerful.

"It's decorative 'motif' Art. Art is perception," Harry tried to rationalize to himself. "The real world ain't art, and never will be. And I'm a real-world kinda guy."

Harry felt Veronica reading his thoughts. Maybe she was, maybe she wasn't. He tried to think more quietly. But she knew what he was thinking, and what he was capable of doing. Maybe she was more whore than secretary. Or maybe even more human being than whore.

Finally, the final chamber, marked by an eye minus pyramid. "Ain't there supposed to be trumpets coming out of the walls, and guys in tights screaming out something in Latin?" Harry said, with his best Rocky Stallone imitation.

Veronica's lips tightened.

Harry quickly continued, with as much "in-the-know" as he could improvise. "I was thinking of some Wagner, Mendelssohn, or maybe Handel."

Harry knew that Wagner wrote the "Apocalypse Now" chopper scene music and that Mendelssohn wrote the wedding march. Maybe he blew the pronunciation of one of the names. If Veronica asked him Opus Numbers or favorite conductors, he'd be dead in the water. Leonard Bernstein was the only conductor he ever really knew, and that was when he was talking about West Side Story on a twenty-year-old PBS rerun.

Veronica leaned over, her ass tight but very firm. She opened the door and turned to Harry. "Good luck, Rex. Break a leg," she said. Her accent was different. Appalachian West Virginia. Not the Harvard-tuned Georgian New South flavor she had at first greeting.

"The Professor was right," Harry thought. "'Class' is all a bluff, a perception. And real honesty is the best bluff of all. So far."

CHAPTER 23

The Hudson River at the 79th Street pier was more sludge than water, but it did give the Professor a view of the sun setting over water. To Professor Jack, a day without giving homage to water or sun was bad karma. There was so much of the real world that he couldn't relate to anymore, but he could still connect with the sun against water. It was the source of his inner vision and the fuel to make it a reality.

An old "George" magazine lay in the trash next to him, featuring its editor, John Kennedy Jr. The Professor had hoped that this Kennedy would have gone into politics, but publishing seemed like a better idea. John-John would lose more than his magazine if the Professor came within ten feet of him. He couldn't talk to Teddy. Another Chappaquiddick would happen, and the whole family would die in the crash next time. Hardball Diamantis would see to that.

It had been thirty years since Jack's fall from grace at the hands of Carlos Marcello and the Illuminati. The Professor still didn't know what members sanctioned his banishment from the world of the living. He knew some of them, but not others. But that was understandable. Jack had only been the President, ignorant of the very existence of positions of far more authority behind the scenes.

A yacht passed by, its sails still glistening in the fading sunlight. There wasn't much about life before the madness that Jack still yearned for, but being able to sail anything he wanted anywhere he wanted still topped the list. The ocean was his domain, and one day he'd return to it. Maybe it would be a Viking's Funeral off Cape Cod. Of course, it would have to be at sunset, and the view of the big open sea at Cape Cod always faces East. But maybe God would be kind and have the sun set in the East, just one time. Such were the Professor's wishes.

The realities floated in amidst the suds of the shoreline surf. The New York Times headline read, "Freefly Multinational Merger Approved by Congress." The Post showed a picture of arch-conservative Jesse Helms and ultra-liberal Jesse Jackson shaking hands with Steven Spielburg. "Partners?" was splashed above the Machiavellian snapshot. The Enquirer featured a story about ancient Templar Masonic Knights, reincarnating to invade the bodies of high-level White House officials. Topping it off, a "Watchtower," announcing the coming of the New Age Apocalypse. Jack preferred his own literary efforts, and his new co-writer, Harry, whom he had sent into the loon's den to make the script happen, had a commonly shared vision.

"Did I put enough in 'Code to Die For' to reach the people? It's my first screenplay, and I'm a novelist. Will it get past the gatekeepers, letter and spirit of the message intact? Is it too late for the truth to make a difference anyway?" The thoughts raced through the Professor's mind. "And what of the human price?" he pondered.

Jack had sent a kid to do a mad visionary's job. Harry still looked forward to experiencing life, and infiltrating the Firefly Organization and the Illuminati was a suicide mission. They always had a way of knowing what was most valuable to you and making it an obligatory part of the deal.

Two hours had passed since Harry had begun his pitch. Three days to go before Jack would recontact him. It was a waiting game now.

A gull circled above, flying more like an eagle over the mighty Pacific than a common scavenger looking for stale donuts. The bird seemed thin, but more contented with flying than eating.

"You look hungry," Jack commented. He tossed what was left of his bread and cracker sandwich up into the sky. The gull swooped in and grabbed a small bite. The pigeons pecking for garbage on the beach got the rest.

CHAPTER 24

"Sometimes the easiest way up a steep hill is straight up," Ross related to Leona, as their mounts made the climb to the mesa above the ranch house.

"I'll fall off this time, I know it," Leona blurted out of her quivering lips. The Appaloosa-Arab steed dug into the sand. "This horse is gonna trip and fall. I know it."

"Not if you don't let him," Ross calmly related. "You don't wanna die, and neither does he. You two will work something out."

"Maybe I should get rid of this shit in the saddlebag. You said we were going out here for lunch, not a pig out with the goddamn Mormon Tabernacle Choir." Leona reached toward the saddlebag.

"Leona, can you do two things for me? "

"Sure, Cowboy Ross."

"Get yer hands away from that saddle bag latch."

"No problem. "

"And SHUT UP!!!" It was the first time Ross had raised his voice to Leona. He really meant it this time.

"Okay. You want me to say 'goshdamnit' instead of 'godammit'. 'Heck' instead of 'hell'. Or maybe 'chut' for 'shit'. 'Fuck' to 'fudge'. Ya really want me to lie like that so you can feel ."

"My wife, Maureen, sang with the Mormon Tabernacle Choir," Ross interrupted.

"And you?"

"She wanted to be a Mormon, and for me to respect her point of view. I'll expect the same courtesy from you."

Leona saw the ocean of pain under Ross' sunbaked face. "No problem, Ross," she said, respectfully.

Leona hadn't been respectful of very much lately, and it felt good even if it was to respect someone else's privilege to feel pain on his own terms.

There was still the matter of the exit from the ranch house. It seemed all too decisive, yet indecisive. There was a finality to it, but toward a very uncertain future.

"We are gonna stop for lunch, right, Ross? And get back to the house before dark? If I don't get my three-minute shower twice a day, I become a real cranky camper."

"Be plenty of time to wash later."

Whatever Ross had in mind, he did have Leona's welfare at heart. Or so she hoped, as she took another look at him against the deep-red canyon rocks.

Ross Cuthand was the quintessential Marlboro Man. Fringed chaps, Mexican spurs, a blue bandanna, and an off-white hat that fit his head like a glove. A Winchester 30-30 bolt-action rifle, complemented by a Colt revolver and a Bowie knife as big as any used at the Alamo. Everything on Ross was authentic, functional, or both.

"Ya know, Ross. I never noticed it. Ever see what people wear in towns or cities? Platform shoes, stiletto heels, tight business skirts that don't let you spread your legs for anybody. And ties. Ya know, I never figured out what a tie was supposed to be for."

"For pulling you along like a dog on a leash, or hanging you up on the highest lamppost." Ross chuckled.

"Or for a game of slave man and vampire mistress over lunch?" Leona offered.

Ross nodded. Not exactly his way of waging war against the Fortune-500 business tycoons who were robbing his country blind, but a start.

The horses reached the plateau. With the exception of the house below and some telephone wires crossing the high plains stubblegrass, it could have been 1860. Leona felt herself scared, then welcomed by the bigness of it all, hardly what she expected.

She smelled wood burning under Ross's hat, a great fire that she had to get close to.

"What are you thinking, Ross?"

"The slave man-vampire Mistress game. It's real popular, even here. The Japanese execs really like it. The more powerful they have to be at work, the more submissive they wanna be in bed. They'd pay mucho dinero to trust someone else to be in control."

"Would you?" The words slipped out of Leona's mouth. "I'm sorry, I didn't mean to . . ."

"Leona. I would give my right arm and left testicle to find a person and situation I could trust. Nothing more I'd like than to take a day off."

"After you take care of business. Men are what they do, and you haven't done what you're supposed to do. Is that it, Ross?"

"Is this a proposal to expand our professional relationship, Leona?"

"You want it to be, Ross?"

"I'll let you know after I take care of business. Which is gonna start just about now. "

Ross pulled out his Winchester and dismounted. Three cars approached the house below: a black limo and two blue and whites.

Panic alarms rang through Leona's head. She stole a glance into the saddlebags. Apparently, Ross was prepared for more than a picnic.

"Dismount, and hold on to the horses, tight!!!" Ross yelled as he grabbed a stick of dynamite from the saddlebag.

"What the hell are you doing?"

"Getting my life back. Yours too."

"News flash, Lone Ranger. Your series has been canceled. They own all the goddamn TV antennas."

"We'll see about that."

Ross lit a long fuse and tossed the first stick.

"What are you doing?! You'll get us both killed."

"Exactly."

Ross's Winchester fired a volcanic blast of thunder that had been brewing for a decade. One shot set it off. The ranch house he spent a lifetime building went up like dry kindling wood caught in a prairie brush fire.

The police circled the building, none brave or stupid enough to enter the inferno.

"We've just died in a great fire, Leona. Then resurrected ourselves up here to the Big Lonesome. Hallelujah." Ross reloaded, then slipped the Winchester back into its saddle holster. He mounted the horse that he loved more than himself, and took one more look at the bridge he had burned behind him down below.

"What about Norma Beth? Your daughter?"

"I sent her away."

"They'll find her. They'll figure out that we didn't die and find her. They'll do what they have to do."

"Not before we do what we have to do. Have you ever moved livestock?"

"Every time I did a trick."

"Cattle and horses are smarter than Johns, Leona. And we'll be holding up in some rough country. Rock-hard trails. Hot days. Cold nights.."

"Let's ride, already," Leona interjected, like a seasoned New York cabbie after a twenty-seven-hour shift, out for one last fare.

Driving Ross's horses and cattle into the mountains was a stupid idea. Four hundred hoofprints were far easier to follow than eight. But Ross wouldn't leave his livestock behind. What did they do to deserve being shot and canned before their time? And what was Ross really planning to do once Hardball Harry Diamantis found out that he had kidnapped his only, and perhaps beloved, daughter?

CHAPTER 25

By high noon, Cuthand's deputies had catalogued the wreckage of the fire. By sundown, the coroner figured out that the charred corpses belonged to John Doe 12 and Jane Doe 135. Official charges of corpse and people kidnapping were slapped on the warrant for Ross Cuthand's arrest. The State of Arizona required 20 years in maximum security if convicted. Hardball Harold demanded a lot more.

"I want him back, I want him dead, and I want my daughter alive!!!" Harold screamed at Ross's next in command, a 26-year-old law school dropout, who figured out that buying a Chief Deputy position was more lucrative than earning a position in the Public Defender's office.

"We're doing everything we can, Mister Diamantis," Kirk Caldwell replied back, calmly.

"He's got my daughter, you moron!!!"

"And this office has surveillance cameras, Mister Diamantis. By order of the Governor and the Supreme Court."

"So, Jake Number 4. You listen to the ACLU instead of me?"

"Mister Diamantis. We are doing everything we can." He glanced outside the glass doors.

Harold's elite corps watched the station from behind their dark sunglasses. The entourage never so much as spit in a Police Station, but knew everything that went on. No cockroach crawled into a coffee cup, and no rat took a nibble out of a donut, without the "circle of four" knowing about it.

Hardball steamed like Mount Vesuvius. "I want Ross Cuthand's head, his balls in his teeth. Or I'll cut you into pieces so small that..." He drew his pocket knife. Kirk backed away, trying to remember everything in the police manuals, hoping that it really worked.

"Mister Diamantis. You are under a lot of stress. I'm sure you don't want to do anything we'll all regret later."

"Screw you, asshole. I'm gonna cut you open, and any other craphead cop who gets in my way, you moron."

Harry took a swing. Blood oozed out of a two-foot-long slit in Kirk's shirt.

Harry locked the door behind him. The goon squad moved in, ensuring that the meeting would stay confidential.

"The cameras are watching us, Mister Diamantis." Kirk had never been in a street fight, and Hardball Harry knew it.

"Fuck the cameras, and fuck you!!!" The blade took out another chunk of flesh and made a hole in the radial artery. Blood spurted across the room.

Kirk fell to the floor, wrapping his sleeve in a tourniquet. Harry offered his assistance.

"Let me help, Jake number gone!!!"

"I need a doctor."

"You need a priest. Confess to me and that camera up there. Confess. How you lived a seven-figure life on a five-figure income. Confess it to me, and the camera. We'll send a free tape to your wife and kids."

"I need a doctor."

"You need to do what I tell you to do, now or you'll die!!!"

Kirk began the confession, starting with the payoffs from the Marcello old guard, the Ultra-right Cuban new guard, and then Hardball's special front organizations. The personal confessions hurt most. The two-day Chicano mistress from personnel. The date with the transvestite whom he framed for cocaine possession. The selling of Mexican whores back to their pimps so he could put his daughter through college.

"Feel better now?" Harry screamed into Kirk's fear-demented face. "You got that?!!!!" he yelled up to the camera.

Kirk pleaded for his life, begging for any mercy he could get from heaven or hell, with Hardball cast as the Almighty and the Devil. It was the look Harry was waiting for. "Mister Diamantis. Please. I need a . . ."

"New start?" Harry whispered, with his trademark sadistic smile. "I'll just push the reset button and . . ."

Harry pulled open Kirk's arm. He laughed as the blood gushed across the room. "A four-footer this time," he boasted to the Circle of Four. "See that?"

Harry aimed Kirk's arm at the camera lens. Whoever or whatever was listening at the other end saw a cloud of red and heard Harold's voice.

"Your blood next time, losers," he declared. "I'm taking it all, and taking down anyone who stops me."

Harry opened the door and tossed Kirk's body on the floor. The cops drew their revolvers. The Circle of Four pulled out their Uzies.

"Gentleman... and ladies," Harry announced dispassionately. "You have six rounds in your guns. We have 150 in ours. That's not healthy arithmetic, is it?"

Harry had more power in his eyes than Rasputin, and more officials in his pocket than Al Capone. The veteran cops knew what he could do. The rookies were afraid of what he would do.

"Your EX-Sheriff Kirk had an accident." Harry turned to Deputy Halson, a family man, who got or went to college on a Marcello-Diamantis foundation scholarship because of high academic achievement at a low-achieving high school in Albuquerque. "Jake number 4, you're Jake number one now. You wanna let my special investigative team out of here, so we can do our work?"

Halson lowered his gun. "He's FBI. Undercover."

"And Sheriff Kirk was the dirtiest cop in the Southwest. Wanted for murder. He just did himself in. Saved the State of Arizona the trouble and expense of a very embarrassing trial. I tried to stop him, but . . ."

"We'll take it from here," Halson interjected.

"We'll be in touch, Sheriff Halson. We now have FOUR very dangerous terrorists on the loose, armed and very dangerous. An old fart and a young corpse, probably somewhere in New York. A Jake number 3 and a young runaway are probably still out there." Hardball gave Halson two sealed envelopes with all the appropriate information. "No one gets kidnapped without my permission," he continued, his voice wavering between the grief of loss and the anger of betrayal. "I want the runaway girl found and brought to me." He stopped himself, anticipating the worst about Leona's ever-shifting loyalties.

Nothing Harry had experienced since stumbling onto Professor Jack had been as he expected. Reality defied stereotype. "This Firefly-Illuminati Board Room is going to be filled with old men with English accents, smoking cigarettes like Nazi SS interrogators," he thought, as the large oak doors closed behind him in the dimly-lit room. "Argentinian bratwurst takes an American holiday. The final 'X-Files' scene, with clones of executive producer Chris Carter running every show with his E.T. girlfriend."

The reality this time was all too much like the nightmarish stereotype. As the lights came up, Harry saw in front of him a large room, built more like a bomb shelter than a place of business. Dark red carpet on the floor, and stark brown walls. A simple oak table, round and solid, with a large chair at each of the twelve stations. On the table, mugs of water, wooden ashtrays, and lots of legal papers. No Masonic symbols or post-Atlantian murals hung on the windowless walls. These people knew who they were. The unholy congregation was dressed in the slickest, hippest, and most expensive warfare attire for the business world; their faces hidden in shadows created by the carefully constructed lights. Most were men, some were women.

Harry checked out the hands of the two female power-brokers. One had thick fingers, the hands not big enough to say "drag queen", but masculine enough to say "power dyke", in the tradition of Golda Meir or Maggie Thatcher. The other had a wedding ring with a diamond the size of a grape, accessorized by fluorescent-violet nails and a long, blond mane flowing over her shoulders, her ample Gen-X cleavage tastefully displayed by a diffused spotlight.

Smoke filled the room, but it was from fine pipe tobacco, not sleazy cigarettes. Harry noticed an ashtray filled to the brim.

"I know you guys don't do your own cleaning in here," he said, to break the ear-shattering silence that optimized intimidation. "How do you get janitorial help these days? 'Blind Are Us' cleaners. Or the kamikaze-special of the week. Cleaning person wanted, ten thousand bucks an hour. Then off with your head for a job well done." He stepped into a spotlight and addressed his hosts in a mock German accent. "I vill give you name, rank und serious number, but I vill not do vindows . . . Then again, you have no windows here."

Harry waited for a reply, something he could fight against or relate to. The silence got louder, screeching in Harry's terrified ears. The head member of the table, a man with a real German accent, addressed him from behind the shadows.

"Rex. I am Hans. We are very interested in what you have been doing and what you have given us." He pushed a copy of "Code to Die For" toward an empty seat, the only one with the lights shining on it. "Sit down, my friend."

"I always like the spotlight," Harry commented as he sat down in a leather-upholstered chair that felt extremely comfortable, from the neck down and, he feared, from the neck up.

"That chair could be yours permanently, if this script turns into the kind of movie we all hope it will be," Hans continued. "Your agent has been very fastidious about seeing that it gets to the top. His efforts were successful. Will yours be, Rex?"

Harry looked over the script. It had "Professor Jack" written into every storyline, but "Harry" into every beat. "It's an adaptation of a novel, 'President Lehman's Express'. I'm glad my agent respected the writing enough to leave it alone."

"You wrote President Lehman's Express?" the power dyke asked.

"What did you like best, the beginning, middle, or the end?" Harry volleyed back. "Which part meant the most to you?"

"The end," Hans replied, on behalf of the group.

"That's the part I like best, too."

"So YOU wrote it, Rex?" the Gen-X representative blew out of her black-lined seductive lips.

"That's me in there," Harry replied. "There's me in here, too," he continued, as he thumbed through the "Code to Die For" script. Harry was honored that Jack let his scribbles, notes, and substories get onto the final draft. The Gen-X underachiever felt like a writer, someone who decides what other people read, think, and even feel. He knew that women at the top were bitches, but he didn't know they could also be hot.

"I also wrote my own music," Harry continued proudly, with a voice directed to Hans, and a smile shown to the Illuminati Vampiress with the big breasts and the glow-in-the-dark nails.

Harry knew he had overstepped the line, but maybe that was the protocol here. Maybe old ex-hippie Neo Nazis liked Gen-X'ers with attitude. The Yuppie creed said greed was good. Advancement by intimidation was the preferred route, and effortless success was the only kind worth any value.

Harry felt something come back from the Vampiress, an instant reward. Then, Hans retorted with instant retribution.

The weapon was pushed across the table to Harry: a vintage Gibson guitar. "Show us what you learned with 'Catfish' in Mississippi, Rex. Or with your agent, 'Backwater Jim'."

"His name is Backwater Jack," Harry asserted, trying to hide the fear that the busker blues he knew wouldn't cut it in the company of people too powerful to even carry cash. "And my music is my own."

"Then tell us what you are about, 'Rex'?" Hans had seen through the bluff, maybe. If he had, it was between him and Harry now.

"Two of these strings are busted," Harry said, as he secretly broke them at the frets.

"Catfish, and probably Backwater 'Jack', could play a guitar with five strings to a crowd of drunken blues fans. You are saying that you can't play with four strings to twelve, no eleven, of the most influential people in the industry. It's a poor teacher who doesn't outdo, or outgrow, his teacher."

"Michelangelo said that," Harry countered defensively.

"And does 'Rex'?" Hans asserted.

Harry sucked it in, then started to play. With the aid of a silent prayer, given to the God whom his mother once believed in, he went to work. His fingers became one with the guitar, each of the strings taking on the job of three. As for the lyrics, Harry went with a song he scribbled down on the trip to Camelot Five. 'Dangerous times then, heroic times now," a few of the descriptors. Then, memories of the good times with Professor Jack, and the bad ones with the desert. "A reality beyond fantasy that became ecstasy," some of the verbage made possible by converting words to lyrics. "The end is the beginning, the beginning the end, and that's where you and I have always been, my friend." The universal words sounded romantic, too. They could be appreciated by listeners trying to get back on good terms with a lover, a friend, a community, or the Godhead. "Wow," Harry said, after the final riff. "I didn't know I was so Black."

He looked up at the all-white, part-oriental congregation, then played them out with a musical coda. No feet tapped along, no hands clapped along, not even a finger moved in time with the music. Even the Vampiress remained still, dispassionate, analytical.

"You must be the kind of audience that's too important to sing, dance, or clap. You enjoy your music with your 'inner ear', right?" Harry directed at Hans.

Harry turned to the Vampiress. "What do you think?"

"Cool," she said, in a tone more corporate than hip.

Harry waited as Hans polled the board for a consensus, addressing each on a first-name basis only. The diction reeked of "elite." Harry had never heard names like Ivan, Yakof, Robert, William, Margaret, or even Kyoto said with so much WASP-ishness. Five affirmative nods of the index finger, two firm "no's," and two passes. It was up to Hans now.

"Rex. We will lend all the support we can to you in the making of 'Code to Die'. You will have a key creative role in the movie and, if all goes well, here. That chair suits you very well. How does it feel?"

"Comfortable? Powerful."

"But you should know that there are two other contenders. You may find yourself working very closely with them. One is a mobster criminal who owns the law. The other is an 'A-line' director whom we brought up out of the farmfield."

"Why are you telling me this, Hans?"

"To make the game more sporting, 'Rex'."

"And what happens to the people who lose the game? Or decide they don't want to play?"

"They become losers. Or much worse."

Harry put on his acting face. "Nothing worse than being a loser. What are the rules of this game?"

"You know them already. Or you'll find them out. Welcome home, Rex." Hans got up, extended his hand to Harry, and led the room in a round of applause. Harry found himself warmed over with a new feeling, pride. But what had he done? He just did what he had to do to stay alive. Was being a survivor the same as being a winner?

The answer came when the door reopened and the board members disappeared. There, in the brightly lit doorway, stood the West Virginian secretary, with an airline ticket and two armed guards. Her mannerisms were warm and very subservient.

Hans stood in the shadows inside the boardroom, his face still hidden from the hired help and the outside world.

"I bet I could have her strip down right here and let me drill her," Harry said to Hans. "With her husband and kids watching."

"And more," Hans commented. "As long as you remember two things."

"One of which is…?"

"The entertainment business is about entertainment, and it is a business."

"With a little global mind control thrown in. Point two?"

"The matter of 'Backwater Jack'. A good student always outgrows his teacher."

"Then dumps him?"

"The Spartans have a saying. Come back victorious behind your shield, or dead over it. Maybe there is enough ancient Greek blood in you to understand that, 'Rex'."

Hans knew more than he was saying. It was a matter of mutual need, Harry thought. Maybe the Illuminati wants to get rich off ticket sales from "Code to Die For." In its obsession with money, the Board of Boards had forgotten that this movie could be a battle cry for a New Revolution where ALL the have-nots revolt against the haves. Was the Illuminati that stupid? Or was it all really just a game, Hans and his committee of ten setting the world against itself, to see who deserves to be the twelfth juror?

Harry felt like a Christian gladiator, but at least the Romans had given him a sword. Could he turn it into a cannon? And who would it blast into oblivion?

CHAPTER 26

Two unwritten rules hung over every regulatory sign at Freefly Studios. "Perception is Reality," and "He who reveals the game destroys himself." Still, they pushed "Code to Die For" into production in record time, with a record budget. A hundred and forty-five million, according to the press releases David personally sent to E.T. and Variety, "compliments", with a closed set to enhance the mystique.

The deal struck with "Rex" was unprecedented. The script would remain intact, all dialogue changes subject to his approval, and he would play the lead. David would direct the star-studded alternative Godfather epic. Everyone from Susan Arquette to Stephanie Zimbalist was slated for a part.

Harry's on-set trailer was larger than any hotel room he'd ever been in. The Five Star room in town was so big that on more than one occasion, he woke up in the middle of the night with a full bladder and couldn't find his way to the can. But the press secretary enjoyed his "follow the yellow brick road" comment about the stain in the 4,000 dollar Persian carpet.

Harry helped himself to another slice of authentic L.A. imitation-New York provolone and looked at his new $800 watch. Ten bells, and still no David. The meeting was supposed to taker place at nine. Maybe Harry was still on New Mexican time. Maybe the watch was all glitter and no gears. Maybe it was the "I made you wait for me" power trip.

But as long as provolone and salami overpacked every compartment in the mini-fridge, Harry could wait a lifetime. Freefly and David contacted him, with the masterful help of his invisible super-agent Professor Jack.

Harry wondered why a 110 page spec script, complete with typos and grammatical errors, had held hostage the most powerful entertainment multinational in North America. It was a good logical first question to ask Davy boy as he sauntered across the set, stopping to eye a sound girl who would never hear of boinking a nouveau rich farm kid, no matter how much clout he had with IATSE.

"Got any coffee, Rex?" David asked. He sprouted a third leg as a stripper-turned-P.A. walked past.

"I'll scoop you out a cup. You probably take your java with fresh cream and extra sugar."

"B-line, Rex. You're supposed to be an A-line writer. And 'java' is dated."

"B-line people are gonna buy tickets to see 'Code to Die For', and inside this trailer, espresso is java. Ya want some, or not? "

"Good come back, Rex."

David helped himself to the homemade brew, which was more ground and filter than coffee.

"We're supposed to shoot today, and I still didn't get my rewrites back, David."

"Late night for the producer, late start for the cast and crew. The way it is in the big time.

"I'm here to make a movie. On a movie set, the director is God. Not the actor, crew, producer, or investors. The director is God. And aren't you the director, Davy?"

David smiled that irresistible grin which wore out reason and melted down cynicism. Harry wasn't buying it. Not anymore. Harry was on a mission, and David was still on a joy ride.

"What's the rush, Rex? You want out of this deal. I can talk to the exec producer. You can be replaced."

"So why did you pay me $15 million? Then keep me away from contacting the outside world? I can't even call out without someone listening in. But it's okay; I talked dirty to the pervert who was bugging the phone. I just hope she's not a guy. If he is, you can tell him that I give homo head over the phone, but nothin' in real life."

"I sense something. You're upset," David said, with a voice pleasant enough to draw you in, and a subtext deadly enough to kill.

"Fuckin' A, I'm upset. Just some things I want to know, David. What do you want to do with me and this script?"

"Structural adjustments and balancing of character tone."

"Carving the meat out of it. Like here." Harry thumbed through the red-inked, cluttered revision, focusing on page 24. He showed David a cleverly placed red mark on page 24. "These phone numbers. I want them like they are. No one buys this '555' crap."

"We can't use the numbers in the script."

"Why not?

"Executive Producer's decision, Rex. No one sees these numbers or names."

"I got a copy of the original script in a locker in Newark, David."

"Do you know who those numbers belong to? We can't put out those numbers to the public, Rex. Some people's access has to be protected."

"Fuck that noise."

"If you knew who those numbers and names belonged to, you'd change the numbers."

"Fuck you, Davy Crockett-boy with a coonskin cap up your ass. The numbers and names stay."

"We'll have to modify the characters. Do some recasting."

"I don't care if you get friggin' Barney the Dinosaur to play the Secretary of Defense. The story stays the same, and the phone numbers don't get changed."

David pondered a moment. A bluff behind the superstar artistic eyes, he thought. He had to call. It was all part of the game, and in David's world, the game had to go on, no matter what the cost.

"You don't know who those numbers really belong to, or you do, 'Rex'." Harry froze. The blank stare again, he thought. He had learned it from an actress doing off-off Broadway, and it never failed him yet. Look at yourself, and you put up a wall that no one can see through unless you flinch.

David sized up his protégé. Would this new discovery thank him? Screw him? Ignore him?

"'Rex?' You're fronting this script for a genius, or you're the biggest find in this town since Orson Wells. If you're headed for the Oscars, I'll be riding your coattails all the way. If it's back down to the gutter, my foot will be the first boot heel on your sorry ass."

"'Code to Die For' is what it is. It is real. It's honest. And so am I, under all the bullshit I gotta do. And underneath all the bullshit you gotta do, maybe you're real, too. Maybe you do know what this script is about."

"Making a buck, staying comfortable, and getting some ass when you can. Like everyone else, Rex."

"Like everyone else used to be, David."

An invisible "huh" slobbered out of David's open mouth. Profound, simple, and completely beyond comprehension.

"Just one more question, David," Harry asked, satisfied with the outcome of the first round. "The ending. You said you had some, ya know, structural suggestions."

Pencils and pens came out. Passion-driven writer/actor had to coordinate with money-obsessed director. A win-win situation for both parties, to get the script shot on schedule and under budget.

"President Lehman gets assassinated. You okay with that, Rex?"

"Sure." Harry helped himself to another block of provolone.

"The mob and multinational bosses kill each other, or go crazy. They don't commit suicide."

"No problem."

"And the main character. The kid crusader. He dies, in a madhouse, not knowing that he's made any difference."

Harry reflected.

"Rex, it was in YOUR draft. In the subtext. You want it in, or not? It's a great dramatic device. He gets activized, effective, crazy, then catatonic."

"Yeah, sure." Harry never had a good poker face and was a worse player. The downward-turned eyes gave him away, once again.

It was all David needed to plan the rest of the game so that the winner would take all, and that winner would be him.

CHAPTER 27

Ross always related to the open sky. It defined the boundaries of his world. Born and raised on the Eastern slopes of the Rockies, he developed a love-hate affair with mountains. The peaks of the ever-steepening hills provided scenery for the ski bums, bunnies, and moguls down below, a scenic backdrop for slow cowboy dreaming in any weather, any season.

Pushing an old herd and a young woman against the clock presented more problems than anticipated. The cliffs and mesas provided protection from the elements and trackers, but they looked more like walls to Ross, closing in on him with every mile into the passes, which were uncharted by even the State Rangers.

Risling National Park was named after its expeditionary force and its leader. Russell Risling was the first white American explorer in the area, an Industrial-Age burnout who thought that the missing sister city of Atlantis was located somewhere in the steep rocks and bottomless canyons. Risling emerged from his first expeditions with manuscripts that astounded his fellow scholars at the University of Chicago. Quicksand swallowed up the second expedition, and at the same time, the Great Chicago Fire burned the parchments.

The tourist information said that the ghosts of the Risling Party remained in the valleys and whispered secrets of the universe to those who would listen. The locals added a UFO connection to boost tourism in a P.R. campaign that eventually backfired. But there were still the formations on the mesa walls.

"They look like people, I think," Leona commented, hypnotized by the jagged rocks that defied gravity. "Like looking up at the stars and seeing gods and ancient spirits. They'd probably talk to you if you were on some really good acid."

"I wouldn't know," Ross countered, hoping that there would be more rocky trail than salt bog ahead.

"Where are we going, Ross?"

"We're ghosts, Leona. We've come here to join the dead."

A cabin emerged from behind the mountains ahead.

"My old hunting lodge," Ross commented. "Built it myself. Didn't tell ANYone about it. Just in case."

"Cool," Leona said, with a smile as wide and as long as Ross' stare.

"We have two options, Leona. We can stay here in Paradise."

"Like Adam and Eve?"

Ross retreated back into himself.

"Don't worry, Ross. I'll let you be Adam, I'll be Eve, and I won't bring home any apples."

"Option number two," Ross continued. "We ride out the other side of this park and find the world. Disappear into it with new lives."

"I tried that, Ross. You can't get rid of your old life by trying to live a new one. Not in the world of people."

"I got a wind generator. The TV used to work once."

"Radio. Music. TV is shit. If I'm gonna be boinking and bopping around in cactus fig leaves, I need my music."

"You mean static, Leona. I didn't figure you for a top forty alternative-Gen-X-individualist."

"And I didn't think you would be afraid of music with some kind of life to it. Ya know?"

Leona noticed a radio in Ross's saddlebag.

"I got some batteries in my electric vibrator, Cowboy Ross. Let's use them." Leona handed Ross the batteries out of the mini-portable, Fujispecial, vibrator stashed in her backpack. "Looks like I won't be needing this anymore."

Leona tossed the Japanese joy toy down a canyon wall. Ross smiled. Maybe it didn't work anyway, or maybe Leona really did fantasize about the same return to Eden that Ross did. In any case, the courtship required musical accompaniment. Ross inserted the 1996 triple, a batteries into his 1965 transistor radio.

"Raindrops keep falling on my head" blared its way through the static. Then something more timely.

"We interrupt this broadcast for a special local announcement. Sheriff Ross Cuthand's body was not yet retrieved from his burning ranch house. But police do know of his whereabouts."

Ross pulled in his horse. Leona held her breath inside her neck. Even the livestock knew it was time to listen.

"Police outside of Phoenix found his daughter, Norma Beth, and her schoolmates. In an unprecedented act of cruelty, just one hour ago, Sheriff Cuthand raped and mutilated his daughter and two of her companions, with "toys" such as branding irons and electric cattle prods. Daughter Norma Beth, the only survivor of today's brutal assault, is officially pressing charges. Meanwhile, Cuthand is suspected to be vacationing somewhere within a hundred-mile radius, with a hooker actively connected to the mob, Hell's Angels, and the infamous Anarchist Delight terrorist organization. Any listeners who know the whereabouts of Sheriff Cuthand are encouraged to call 555-1453."

"We can call in a request!" Ross commented.

"'Ironic'. Ya know, by Alanis Morrisette?"

Leona was never in more danger, yet she never felt more protected.

Ross knew the value of being honest with the facts, but not about his emotions.

"Yer scared?" Leona asked, hoping that the answer would be "no," but knowing it was "yes."

"They won't find us here. And Norma Beth wasn't anywhere near Phoenix today. They're calling me out by trying to take my honor. What I value most."

"They always try to take what you value most," Leona commented. "Are you going to let them take me, so you can keep your honor?"

Ross tried to retreat back into himself. Every time he tried to address this big new question with time-honored answers, he only became more confused. Though he lived in a climate that changed every ten minutes, his views, perspectives, and moral guideposts remained unchangeable. That internal compass kept him on course, as long as he set sail in the desert.

All of that was changing now. For the first time in his life, Ross felt lost, in the middle of the land he knew like the back of his hand.

"What are we gonna do, Ross?" Leona asked.

"Keep moving. Keep fighting. Stay alive." Ross had a plan in mind, one that had been incubating for years. Finally, he would have the chance to implement it. Marshall Matt Dillon and Dirty Harry had no chance against Hardball Harry Diamatis' empire. But there was one consolation. "Daddy Dearest" had given Leona and Ross the greatest gift possible, a life sentence to the outlaw trail, fighting a final battle against primal evil.

CHAPTER 28

The Professor had contemplated the question again and again in his weary mind, as he stood on the corner of 5th and 50th. Maybe the invisible voice behind the Confessional inside St. Paddy's Cathedral could give him a truthful answer, or at least one he could use. Moral dilemmas remained easy on the spirit for people without conscience, and didn't tax the cranial vault for those with little intelligence. But Professor Jack's heart and mind had grown since he met Harry, in ways he had never bargained for.

Most of the other "post-assassination" sons Jack had adopted dropped out of sight; some ran away, a few called in the Feds to make a deal. Most were pulled out from under him, like faithful horses in battle who died out of exhaustion, an enemy bullet, or sheer neglect.

Harry stuck with him for all this time. But could Professor Jack stick with Harry? Would the mission be served by informing its young front-line commandos about its real danger and consequences?

Harry was now swimming with Hollywood sharks. In New York, the unwritten rule is that you tell people you're gonna screw them over, then you screw them over. In L.A., the sharpest knives come from the weasel with the widest smiles. "Code to Die For" made Harry a Prince in the kingdom he was sent to destroy.

Professor Jack opened the massive Cathedral doors and caught a glimpse of a bus going up Fifth. "NYC to L.A., $100 Return," the Madison Avenue ad read, amidst the Lower West Side graffiti. "It might as well be a hundred million return," the Professor thought as he rechecked his pockets, hoping that the dime he felt a few blocks ago was really a quarter.

The Professor's revolutionary war chest had hit rock bottom, for good this time. Carlos Marcello's "deep throats" had kept him alive with drop-off survival money for three decades. If Professor Jack starved, it would be no fun. Better to let the ex-President live with a full stomach and an empty spirit. Denying the most energetic President of the 20th century food in his stomach was nothing. Denying him access to the game, the sport, the grand endeavor of shaping history was a far more vicious punishment.

But punishment for what? For banishing Marcello to Guatemala in the heat of the Kennedy vs. mob wars in the early 60s? For screwing up the Cuban situation in so many ways? For trying to get young Americans not to accept their limitations? For discovering the Illuminati's real connection to the White House? Professor Jack still was not sure of what that connection was. Maybe the whole thing was a dream, anyway. It all happened so long ago, so far away. Nothing was the way it was in '63.

But one thing Professor Jack remembered was that he was Catholic. As long as St. Patrick's Cathedral stood defiantly against the wind, rain, and graffiti artists, the roof on the Stock Exchange wouldn't fall down on 97% of the world's population.

Melting down one pillar or three icons could feed every hungry stomach from Times Square down to Battery Park for a week. But the destitute masses still needed gold and silver-lined likenesses of Heaven to keep faith in a benevolent God alive. "East India puts more money into making music than bread," Jack thought. "It's drama that keeps people awake, not reality. Make people believe in the drama, and they will change reality," he pondered, hoping that there would be enough of "Lehman's Express" and Harry, in 'Code to Die For,' to make it work.

The Professor knelt, crossed himself, then reached into his pocket. He could spare a stale Hershey bar for the poor box. Someone needed it more than he did, maybe.

The Confessional booth looked the same as it always had. It felt familiar, safe. Just like Catechism days, at a time when a feared hoodlum was a Southy who tossed eggs at the Bentley on Halloween. When pain was a bruised knee on a New England football field, and a slapped face from a cheerleader who really did mean "no".

The Priest took his position, asked the usual questions, and heard one of the usual questions.

"Father, does God allow you to do evil in the cause of good?"

"God's ways are moral, and if you are doing evil things, maybe you are not doing God's will." The response was cold, textbook, and went straight into Jack's heart.

"No, Father. You don't understand."

"Could you be more specific? If you tell me more about what's bothering you, God can help you."

The Professor's throat clammed shut. The air felt tense, like it was closing in around him.

Maybe he was being followed. Maybe St. Patrick's was not the refuge it used to be. It would not be the first time the Confessional was used to extract information for very secular means. Every clandestine organization in the world, from the CIA to Interpol, had used the Confessional to extract information they needed.

Still, the Professor had to take the chance. His personal revolution was about the Universal Heart now, not just world politics or settling the score with old mob bosses. He had to know what the war was about now, what could be gained by continuing the fight, and what could be lost.

"Can we talk about Jesus, instead of me?" The Professor asked. "This is His house, isn't it? His life reflects ours, or at least should."

"You sound like a smart man."

"Intelligence is a gift God gave to me. It would be a sin not to use it. Correct, Father?"

A delay. Once again, the Professor had forgotten that his lightning-quick mind was better at shooting down enemies than at getting him friends, and he needed a friend more than another notch on his gun.

"I'm sorry, Father," the Professor slurred out, slipping down into apology. "I have a mind that doesn't stop."

"Maybe you should speak from your heart, and not your intellect."

Jack smiled. He could feel it being heard at the other side of the wall. Either this Confessor was a well-trained Jesuit, who had perhaps spent some off time in the Bowery and a Tibetan Monastery, or he was the wisest interrogator Marcello, Diamantis, or the Illuminati ever sent his way.

"The truth shall set you free, Father."

"It has for centuries." The Priest knew enough not to call Jack "Son." A small thing, but an important one. But small things seemed to be more important than big ones for Jack these days.

"Jesus was a revolutionary, true or false?" Jack's words were Professorial, his subtext very human.

"True."

"A 'what's in it for us' kind of guy, Father. True or false?"

"True. But He was also the Son of God."

"And Jesus fought against a 'what's in it for me' kind of world. True or false?"

"True. Love requires you to think beyond your own immediate needs."

"So, Jesus' allies, followers, and friends were 'what's in it for us' kind of people. True or false, Father?"

"Are you talking about the disciples? They were ordinary men."

"But they were 'what's in it for us' kind of guys. What's good for someone else is ultimately good for me. What goes around comes around. They knew that love is the highest form of self-interest."

A delay, then an all-too-familiar reply. "I don't understand what you are trying to say."

"Okay, Father. Simple."

"Direct."

"From the heart. Jesus put his disciples through hell. He made them leave their families, their homes. Most of them got crucified. None of the Apostles got a comfortable retirement on Crete after putting in a solid career serving the Lord and spreading the Gospel."

"And . . ."

"The question, Father. Jesus made the most selfless people he could find go through the most pain, for the cause of his Spiritual Revolution."

"For GOD'S spiritual revolution."

"But was Jesus sure of that? Didn't Jesus have lingering doubts about himself, the world, and even God, until the time of dying on the cross?"

A delay, then a truthful answer. "I don't know."

"But, Jesus went on anyway, right? Pulling Jewish schleps out of their comfortable homes and making them into fire-breathing Christian revolutionaries. So they can make it a 'what's in it for us' kind of world."

"And."

"The person who feels the vision has the obligation to make the people he cares most about suffer most, for the sake of the revolution. He puts himself and his friends through hell because he and they are 'what's in it for us' people. If recruit "A" balks at busting ass for the revolution, then it means that he's not part of the revolution. He's part of the problem, not the solution. The real revolutionary has the obligation to abuse that recruit. If the recruit gets killed fighting for the revolution, he becomes one of its martyrs. If he were a 'what's in it for me' kind of guy, he was part of the problem, and you killed off one of the enemy with your opponent's own bullets. It means that a revolutionary has the obligation to abuse as many people as he has to for the sake of the revolution, even if your recruits are dedicated revolutionaries in the beginning. If they run out of strength, faith, patience, or morals in the middle of the battle, and want to go home, they become counter-revolutionaries. And then, if anything happens to them, it's not your fault."

Jack stopped. He knew that he had lost the Priest ten thoughts ago, but he had to verbalize it for himself. Still, he wanted some kind of answer.

"It's a new idea, or maybe an old rationalization, Father. Was Jesus morally justified in telling his Apostles that he loved them? Jesus made them feel good about themselves, then hooked them into lives where they'd suffer more than even he did."

Another pause. It was one of those questions so basic to the human condition that the Priest had never been asked it. "Is this about you, Jesus, or God?"

"All three, maybe," Jack replied. "I am an Ex-Catholic."

"No such thing. True or false, my son."

"True, Father."

St. Peter's Assistant Prosecutor allowed Jack to plea-bargain. "Go in peace and sin no more. Ten Hail Marys, and five Our Fathers, but with a catch. You have to think about what the words mean this time. Think about them with your heart."

"You drive a hard bargain, Father."

"God's law can be hard for those who carry with them the sin of pride."

"Or freedom? The only way to serve Jesus is to outdo him. Try to be more loving, giving, and courageous than He was, or could be."

Professor Jack's wit won him the match. It was a victory he did not want to win. Whatever task he took on during that blurry winter of 1963, he was now obligated to finish. Innocent blood would have to be shed to make the Vision happen. He prayed with all his might that it would be his.

CHAPTER 29

"I put three hundred million real bucks into your hundred and ten mil production. When I want to talk to the star, I talk to the star!" Hardball's Brooklyn scream pounded through the receiver, but to no avail.

"Rex is in rehearsal with the director," Second Assistant Director Carole Steinberg replied in a soft, even tone, designed by both intent and accident to frustrate any attempt to contradict her. She was a product of selective engineering, daughter to a nouveau-rich Brooklyn bookie-turned stockbroker and a New Hampshire harp virtuoso, with bloodlines back to the American Revolution. "If you would like to leave a message for Rex, I can be sure that he....."

"Listen, you bitch. my people said that this asshole is masquerading as the best actor in Hollywood."

"An interesting trick, Sir. If he's masquerading as the best actor in Hollywood, and everyone believes him, then he must be great. Worth every penny he's been paid." A brave move, boldly executed, while she wrote down the number on the call display.

"And where does a $100 a day P.A. get off calling a ten-million-dollar artist Rex? He's gotta have a last name."

"Not according to any record I have."

"His legal contract? Passport? Driver's license."

"Sir, that's none of my..."

"Come on. What's with this "Rex" thing? Is he a damn New Age model? A fag who's too sensitive to have a last name? A Nigger rap screamer who painted himself white to hide from a possession charge? The first step toward trusting someone is knowing their name. Don't you think?"

"I don't know Rex's name, Sir."

"Mine's Harold. What's yours?" Harold asked, in a voice as inviting as a marriage proposal to a 50-year-old, 350-pound spinster.

Carole remembered that the big 35 was a few days away. The only thing she had to show for three and a half decades of powerplaying was an empty bed, a career well behind schedule, and a kitchen full of cats. "Carole Steinberg," she answered, indulging in the hope that the fire-breathing dragon on the other side of the phone might be her knight in shining armor.

"Carole, with a C and an E?"

"Yeah, my mother thought it would be classy and my father thought it would be.." She felt the indifferent silence at the other end of the phone, then heard the infamous Hardball laugh. The trap shut tight on her foot, the boom ready to chop off her head.

"Listen up, Carole with a C and an E, you dried-up, Jew-WASP piece of shit. Someone in my organization told me that I should have a face-to-face with this superstar kid you got. See if he's worth fifteen million of MY dollars."

"I'm sorry, Sir. I'm not allowed to…"

"Here's what you're gonna do. You're gonna put me on the phone with this wonder kid, or ship his ass out to where I am. Then I'll decide if I'll have you promoted, fired, or serving kaska to horny old men in a Saudi steam bath."

The threat sounded real. No cleverness. No protocol. Carole could outmaneuver passes, marriage proposals, and paying back business debts. But direct confrontation terrified her. As a bookworm better at learning than catfights, she'd avoided human conflict her entire life. Being a power bitch was a skill learned only after she got her summa cum laude degree at the UCLA film school. Hardball was a born master at using power to intimidate and outmaneuver his opponents.

"Get me the damn Director, you worthless bitch," Hardball repeated.

A moment of reflection, reaction, and response. 'I'll get him, Sir," Carole replied. Her head said it was good business. Her heart said it was another link in a chain that was her life, an existence in which she learned to accept her limitations.

"Thank you," Harold replied, with the cordiality of a headwaiter in a five-star restaurant.

Carole pressed the button reserved for only insiders, the one that led to Rex's trailer, where the blueprints for the biggest romantic-political thriller of the decade were being constructed, line by line.

Within fifteen seconds, David grabbed the phone. "Hello. David here," he announced boldly, as if proclaiming a national holiday.

"I wanna talk to my investment," Hardball demanded, in a voice barely louder than a whisper.

"You're talking to him," David replied, impressed once again with his own wit.

"Get that shit-eating grin off your pig-ass eating lips. Where's Rex?"

Harry knew from the first phone ring that his father had found him. Over the last three years, he could feel Hardball Harold coming from a mile away. After sharing his life with the Professor, the young Harry's radar was a hundred times better. But were his instincts?

Harry shook his head as David handed the phone his way. The young Harry had changed his face, walk, and talk, but not his voice. Even if he did his gruffest Richard Nixon, his whiniest Richard Simmons, or his gayest Steven Urkel, Hardball would hear his son Harry underneath it.

"Rex? Is that you, kid?" Harold said. "I hear great things about you. You brought in a billion-dollar script, and you're gonna do a trillion-dollar job."

Even David could see the fear in Harry's eyes. Something about Hardball scared the shit out of the wonderboy, who scared the shit out of everyone in Hollywood. It was leverage, and, true to form, David used it to get under the belly, rather than claw his way on top.

"He's indisposed," David said into the receiver.

"Taking a shit? I do my best negotiating when I'm taking a dump. It's one of the real things that we guys can still enjoy without a woman screwing it up. Put him on."

"Mister Diamantis. Rex is…"

"Great, fantastic, the best," Harry interrupted, with a desperate million-dollar imitation of a $50 Vegas hooker.

"Is he giving it to you up the ass, or in the mouth?" Hardball asked, brimming with pride for the surrogate son who would make him billions at the box office.

"Rex is filling every opening in our bodies. Me and my four sisters are getting gassed up from Rex's power juice in the front tank, the back tank, and under the hood. Mmmmmmmmmm." Harry could feel himself getting an erection, the nipples on his chest blowing up like balloons and getting sucked dry.

"You girls take care of Rex, and Uncle Harry here will take care of you."

Harold couldn't have been prouder. "Whoever has the stickiest hand, take the phone and give it back to Davy boy."

David took back the phone. He had at least one foolproof blackmail scheme to ensure that he made money and looked good, at the cost of his competitors. He had already hired a transvestite to come on to Rex, photograph the night of wild passion, then blackmail the wonderboy. Rex would get paid fifteen million by the studio to be in his first starring role on the big screen. David would demand back 45 million to keep the Oscar-winning newcomer's picture out of the tabloids. The 30 million would go back into David's own private production company, or into a deal to get Rex for three more features as an investor. An old kickback trick, but an effective one.

David saw even bigger opportunities. As usual, it was about finding out what people wanted, then giving it to them at the highest price you could get. Rex wanted to keep away from Hardball, and, for reasons of passion, fame, or defiance, to make "Code to Die For." Hardball Diamantis wanted "Code to Die For" to be the next "Citizen Kane," and his adopted offspring, "Rex," to be the new Orson Wells.

A wise snake takes the most torturous route from A to B toward its goal. And that goal was to occupy the upcoming vacancy in the Illuminati High Command. Official word was that Hardball Harry and David were the contenders. Unofficial rumor was that "Rex" had all the makings of a Multinational Dictator, too.

But there would be room for only one more demagogue on the Board of Boards. David would have to outdo Rex and Hardball Diamantis. There was much glory to be had in the making of 'Code to Die For'. If done David's way, it could ensure a lifetime role for David in the committee that called ALL the shots in Hollywood. If done the way Rex and his anonymous ghost writer-agent envisioned, it could spell the end of David's acting, or perhaps living, career.

But David sensed a very powerful and possibly unwilling ally in his corner. Whoever wrote the original draft of "Code to Die For" had conscience and intelligence. There was guilt behind each heroic line. Those attributes always came with a compulsion for self-sabotage. That self-sabotage was the ultimate Achilles heel for Rex, his invisible agent, and the script they seemed to value above life itself.

CHAPTER 30

Horse stealing in the Old West meant hanging. Car theft in the new one carries a minimum of six months behind bars. Either one was lethal to a man like Ross Cuthand.

It usually took Ross a week to get used to a new Patrol car. He never pushed a vehicle past its limits. With the five-and-a-half cylinder Buick LeSabre he stole from the Taco Bell parking lot, while Leona pretended to be a dumped Long Island tourist looking for the whereabouts of her fiancé, he would have to violate that rule.

The engine choked with every crank of the drive shaft to maintain the unofficial 70-mile-an-hour speed requirement on Route 66. The gauge indicators hung loose off the scale, listening more to wishful thinking or levitating thoughts than to what was going on under the hood.

"Ross, you could have stolen a Beemer. A Jag. Even a damn TransAm," Leona screamed out through gritted teeth.

"And get pulled over," Ross related. "In the Old West, the smartest cowboys rode the plainest horses. Brown, blacks, nothing fancy. And nothing too fast."

"And nothing too reliable?" Leona commented. The engine generated yet another mystery sound, ticking down its inevitable demise. "How much further?"

"A few hours."

"What's a few? Three, twenty, a hundred and thirty-seven?"

"Two."

The road sign ahead fulfilled Ross's promise. "St. Louis, Kansas, 100 miles."

Leona's heart dropped into her stomach. "We're going to St. Louis, Missouri. That's gotta be another, what, four hours?"

"An hour and a half in rush hour."

Leona froze, as if a prisoner whose indefinite reservation on death row had been commuted to ninety minutes.

"We have to do this," Ross commented.

"But it's hard."

"Most things that you have to do so you can get where you have to are hard."

"And easier if you have a friend with you?" Leona looked at Ross's sky blue eyes, desperately hoping for protection, friendship, and understanding.

"I did what I had to do at the time, you did what you had to do. You were under the influence. I, for the first time in a long while, wasn't."

Ross didn't have to elaborate on the way Leona carved Nathan Williams into shreds to please Daddy Dearest. She knew that she was under the influence of powerful drugs and a father who had the kind of spell that would make Rasputin look like a five-and-dime amateur hypnotist.

She finally felt responsible. At first, for everything, then for a few key transgressions over the years, which she knew she shouldn't have done. She was sober, on her way to being clean, now. But getting clean in a dirty world remained the most dangerous way to stay alive.

"Ross, why did you send the box I took from Nathan back to his mother, without opening it?"

"Because Nathan asked me to, under his breath. A last request."

"When?"

"While your soul was sleeping. Your knife was carving your father's initials into his rib cage, from the inside."

Leona sank into her seat. Maybe she had it coming, maybe she didn't. "We don't need to bother Nathan's family about it. There are other ways to get my father in jail, and get my brother Harry back from wherever he's at."

"True, Leona. But there's one more player in this game. One more person that this is all about."

"That old geezer who thinks he's Kennedy?"

"Whether he thinks he's JFK, or whether he is JFK, it doesn't matter much. He's being JFK. Making things happen in places where things are not supposed to happen."

"You figure all this out?"

"After Nathan whispered something to me in street Mexican. While you were making bacon strips out of his…."

"Okay!!! I'm sorry, okay? I'm really, really sorry."

"So is Nathan's ghost. Unless we can get back the box and figure out what he really died for. A man has the right to have his death mean something."

"So does a woman," Leona thought, but didn't say. She would have to tell the honest kind of lies from here on in. An honorable outlaw on a trail not yet blazed, or even defined.

The Burger Palace experience in Kansas City tasted just like L.A., New York, or Detroit, even though the cattle grazed on pastures twenty miles out of town and the slaughterhouse was three blocks down the street.

Leona wasn't hungry, but she ate anyway. She took small, nervous bites, intended to keep her mouth and senses busy with things external. It took her mind off the internal turmoil in her newly found soul. The boxes for the "make them how you want them" quarter-pounder giganto burgers were all the same yellow-tinged white plastic. They reminded her of the box Nathan would never open for her. Hardball Harry had assigned her the job of finding out whatever information she could from Nathan, in the most effective way possible. Even after he came into her with a volcanic eruption of love juice that had been bottled in for years, name, rank, and favorite neurosis were all he came out with. Hardball already knew about Professor Jack's eccentricities. So did most everyone else within a hundred miles of Younger Rapids, New Mexico.

The box entrusted to Nathan by the Professor was a good luck thing. Jack had made Nathan promise to never open it until he got home, or "to the other side." A gift from a lunatic to his protector, and a promise Nathan was obliged to uphold. Besides, maybe Professor Jack was an Apache Sorcerer, testing Nathan's strength of character. Tales of Native witchcraft haunted urban expatriates, in part because they were very real.

Leona had seen it in other middle-aged burnouts, Willy Lomans of all creeds, colors, and sexual preferences. It seemed childish at the time, so she let him have his way. Besides, Nathan had left the motel room with no forwarding address except "a better place."

Leona glanced at her reflection in the freshly shone vinyl. Deadness overtook her, like a tidal wave from the Blackest waters of hell. Then, a stranger emerged from the men's room.

"Leona, you ready?" he said, in a familiar-sounding voice. He carried a large plastic bag packed with clothing, a look of finality in his eyes.

"Ross?" she said, noticing the blue color inside the black portholes and the pale-white cheeks.

Ross had raised a mustache when he was 15, a full beard by his 18th birthday. Fads came and went, but Ross's facial growth remained full. The hairy wall he hid behind was rumored to have blood vessels in it. If a razor were to ever touch it, he would bleed to death. So his friends joked, and so, in time, Ross began to believe.

"Cowboy Ross?" Leona said, noticing his new wardrobe, featuring Dockers, a striped shirt, an imitation polyester tie, and a blue blazer.

"Yeah. It's me," Ross muttered out of a face that didn't feel like his own, in an accent which was becoming increasingly generic.

"How do you feel?"

"Naked? But maybe you have to feel naked sometimes."

"You know, you're an introvert. It's dangerous for introverts to get rid of the hairy walls on their faces."

"Then I'll just have to be an extrovert. I always wondered what it would be like, facing life naked. Jump in the pool, sink or swim. So, do I look... different?"

"Unrecognizable, Ross. And younger."

"Really?" Ross found himself saying, with a smile he never expected to show, or had seen.

"What's in the bag?" Leona asked.

"Something for you."

Ross showed Leona the business suit with a pH 7 all around. A middle-of-the-road outfit for generic people. Bright, sunshine colors with severe, industrial lines.

"It's perky, Cowboy Ross. Straight out of a 1963 Disney movie. A damn Doris Day Original. Am I really supposed to wear this?"

"And this."

The blonde wig didn't have anything crawling or growing in it. It even looked new. But something about the style and texture gave Leona the shudders.

"What's wrong? Just try it on. No one here's watching."

"Ross."

"Please, just try it on. You can't be recognized either."

"Maybe you recognize this." Leona slipped the wig on. "Your daughter. Just like she always kept her hair, in high school and Bible camp. Through good and hard times and the bad, good times and the sad," she continued in a mock Western accent. She shook her head with a cheerful Charlie's Angels giggle, gave Ross the dirtiest look he'd seen in a dog's age, and reached behind her head to pull the blonde rug off her aching head.

A police car zoomed outside. Ross pushed Leona's arm back with his left hand, then gripped a sharp steak knife with his right.

"You keep that on you, or I'll shave you bald and glue it on. You read me!"

Finally, Leona saw the look in Ross's eyes. He was a good man, but underneath it all, still a man. And when pushed, all men were cruel, at least in Leona's world. They also couldn't handle the naked truth about matters of the heart.

"Is that what happened with your ex-wife? And that other daughter you never talk about? Did you shave them bald because they were bad?"

Ross retreated. The hidden button had been found and pushed hard. "It was a long time ago. We were different people. I was getting it from all ends, from the criminals, the cops, the victims, and the mayor. I couldn't handle getting it from home."

"Getting what?"

"No respect. I give people 180 percent respect, and I expected something back. At least at home. I tell myself that it all went bad when I started drinking, but the ghost of self-sabotage has many faces."

Leona paused. Best to let Ross stew in the darkness of his own skeleton-infested closets for a moment. "Was it like an S and M thing? She wanted pain, you gave it her her?"

"She was going through therapy. I should have been."

"Did you give them wigs?"

"Huh?" Ross replied, woken up from a trace, and out of a place that he thought was buried and gone.

"Wigs, Ross. I knew a guy who got off on shaving the head of every new girlfriend. Especially the ones he really liked. They all said yes to it. And he gave them all real good wigs."

Ross sighed.

"It was just hair, Ross. It did grow back on her, didn't it?"

"So I'm told," Ross replied.

"And you didn't like to cut up anything that bleeds. Right?"

"So I'm told. So I remember, at least."

"So, we're even?" Leona extended her hand, outstretched, palm up, eager to receive whatever Ross wanted to pour into it.

"Even." Ross put his fingers in the palm, squeezing Leona's hand as tight as he could. As tight as he dared to.

CHAPTER 31

"The ending. It has to be on target, like his death means something. Something bigger than even his life." Harry hadn't slept for 96 hours and had enough energy to go another 200, as long as he didn't stop to rest or slow down to warp speed. "The main character in 'Code to Die For' takes his final exit by spontaneous combustion. Mass becomes energy and kaboom, big bang revolutionizes the whole damn universe as we know it, and as he knew it."

"Rex, this is a political gangster movie. We can't do 'Godfather goes Naked Lunch' with time warp." Assistant Producer Carole Steinburg was prepared to read Harry chapter and verse, in the "rules of spontaneous creativity" manual imprinted on her UCLA-trained mind. "Good drama follows story structure rules."

"Creative fire has no rules," Harry countered. "If I'm wrong, you can hang me with that power scarf so tastefully wrapped around your pseudo-liberal red neck."

"That's supposed to be funny?"

"No, it's supposed to be true. Because it is true."

Carole looked to David. He had refereed countless disputes between people with money and people with talent. This time, David just wanted to see how it would happen. But with nearly a billion dollars riding on 110 minutes of movie, Carole demanded something tangible from wonder-boy director David Deitrick.

"Carole, Rex's character is on the edge of dying. A life and death existence. Maybe like Rex himself." David smiled. Like always, he let the truth speak for itself, then used it for his advantage. "All the best artists did their best work when they were flirting with death. Mozart. Beethoven. Jonathan Winters."

"Jim Morrison. Marilyn Monroe. Hendrix. John Belushi," Carole countered. "Is our star going to finish this movie alive?"

"If he dies, you won't have to pay him, Carole," David shot back.

"I'll just collect next lifetime," Harry volleyed out. "With a price of dying tax."

"That's not funny," Carole fired back.

"It wasn't supposed to be," Harry interjected. "But the rest of the script is. The funniest comedy, the deepest drama, and the most in-your-face, no bullshit political satire since 'The Graduate,' 'Catch 22,' 'Goodfellas,' and light years ahead of 'Pulp Fiction'."

"He's right," David added. "You've seen the dailies. And the revised script."

"Yeah. Great beginning. Gripping middle. I just don't know about the ending." Carole had as much to lose as anyone else if 'Code to Die For' failed with the box office popcorn eaters or the brandy-sipping critics.

Harry's bloodshot eyes burned like hot coals, and his eyelids felt heavier than the earth itself, but he knew he couldn't go to sleep. The ex-street kid who could barely pick up the subtext of a B-video promo ad really was wiser, livelier, and funnier than Orson Wells in his 'Citizen Kane' days. The Ancient Guides possessed Harry's body, mind, and spirit now. Maybe they would give them back to him. Maybe not. But there was no way that Harry would emerge from the Magical Mystery Ride the same.

"What's the face of real enlightenment?" Harry felt himself proposing. "The face you get when you know what it's all about, then become what it all should be about." He looked into a mirror. "What frame is happening around these eyes that keep changing color on me? Is it a long, white beard, a cross between Jerry Garcia, Willie Nelson, and Moses? A skull and crossbones? Or maybe bushy eyebrows, a mustache, and a cigar. Groucho. Or Einstein. Maybe Groucho and Einstein were the same guys, ya know? They had to be."

Harry improvised a Grouchoesque version of the theory of relativity. David laughed. Carole took notes. Harry just kept going. He was on firm footing as long as he kept flying. Besides, it was a once-in-a-lifetime opportunity, passed up only by those possessed with fear or sanity.

CHAPTER 32

In Professor Jack's pockets, change for three local phone calls. Between his ears, a trillion-dollar agenda. As a logical man, Jack had no choice but to go shopping.

The West Side JFK Memorabilia Auction attracted a new class of movers and shakers. Armed with newly-issued American Express Gold cards and a velvet-Elvis taste for fine art, these nouveau riche fit well into the Fourth Reich. So did Hardball Harold Diamantis.

Hardball arrived at the 79th Street Auction late enough to sit in the back and remain inconspicuous. It was a gift he still maintained from his days of being a street cop, then a back-alley gangster.

"The suckers sit up in the front," he commented to the man in the black chauffeur suit and pitch black sunglasses next to him. "You bring in one of those walking stiffs?" Hardball continued, sure of his current social superiority, but seeking companionship from his former caste.

The chauffeur remained silent.

Hardball took a whiff of air, then offered some heartfelt advice. "Hey, I don't wanna get personal or nothin', but you smell like shit. Ever think of taking a shower?"

"Every time I try, the stench of walking stiffs stays on me," the black-suited man said, with the manner of a person well above the station of his attire.

"Do I know you?" Hardball asked.

"Not anymore," the man answered.

Hardball did a double-take. His logic was checkmated, then diverted into a box canyon. He had crossed many people on his way up to the top. Could the stranger in black be one of them?

"I just came to watch the auction," Professor Jack continued, his New England accent well hidden under a Southwestern drawl. "I do what I have to do to keep my family fed. My boss does what he has to do to keep his mistress happy."

"And who is his mistress?" Hardball inquired, without missing a beat.

"A very stupid and beautiful lady, and a very buyable one," Jack fired back.

"The best kind," Hardball added, as he eyed the women in the front rows, looking past the Jackie-O outfits into their pathetically desperate faces. One of them would be his for the night, or the rest of her lifetime. Both were usually the same duration during Hardball's babe-hunting season.

The gavel banged. The auction started. JFK books. Lamps. China. Then a desk.

"A special item," the auctioneer boldly announced. "The very desk where President John F. Kennedy formulated the solution to the Berlin Crisis.

"Bullshit," Jack reflexively spat out. "That crisis was solved on the crapper, in the middle of a major league shit." His accent lost its twang.

Hardball turned to Jack. "Hey, 'Tex', what's your game?"

"Same as yours," Jack remembered the Cuban Missile Crisis, as best as his mind could recall it. A fair bluff is as good as a good punch as long as you stay in character.

Hardball gives the Professor a very non-academic stare, learned on the streets and perfected in the school of hard knocks. It was a textbook "I see through you" laser, designed to burn a loser stupid enough to believe in honesty, or a fool desperately trying to hold on to his nerve.

The Professor experienced something odd and frightening. What was it all about? Was the whole JFK thing a dream? Was he really who he said and believed he was? He had to be bold. He had to be Presidential.

He had to give Hardball Harold nothing. It was the only way a man like Harold would ever respect him.

Fate sent a referee, in the form of a waitress with a tray of imitation beef pigs in a blanket and imported California wine. She was pleasing to look at and an innocent bystander. Spoils of war would go to whoever won the battle of wills that had established itself.

Hardball gulped down two glasses, showing off how he could hold his liquor. The Professor nibbled on a hot dog, desperately avoiding the temptation to swallow the whole thing into his very empty, churning stomach.

"Are you one of us, or one of them?" Hardball asked his black-suited opponent, maybe a friend.

"I know the rules. If you're one of 'them', then there are two ways to survive. Kiss ass or kick ass."

"And if you're one of 'us', Tex?"

"Keep the crowd entertained. Keep them laughing. Or keep them hostage, with technology or power. As long as they think you have a skill they need, which they don't have, you stay alive. But a bullshitter always gets crapped on before he's hung, and he always gets hung."

Hardball had never had the riot act read to him so coldly and directly. This chauffeur was definitely in the driver's seat. But of what car, and on what mission? It had to be Professor Jack. And he was armed with much more than madness and self-righteousness. There were no other options available.

"Later, Tex?" Harold waited and watched.

"Your court, my rules." Jack felt like himself for the first time in thirty years. He extended his hand to Hardball. "May the best asshole win."

"I'm a bigger asshole than you'll ever be," Harold sneered.

"No doubt," Jack replied, slipping back into the monastery of nobility.

"Your father was a gangster. He's probably turning over in his grave."

"No doubt."

Another tray made the rounds. Red wine this time. The two adversaries toasted each other. Red wine passed over their parched lips. It tasted like blood to the gangster outlaw in the black hat and the visionary sheriff in the hole-ridden white one.

CHAPTER 33

"Grief is a personal thing. Everyone handles it different," Ross Cuthand said to Leona by way of reminder, as he rang the doorbell on the house Nathanial William clung to as a timid child, stayed away from as an adventurous adolescent, then yearned for as a burnt-out adult.

The one-story-plus-attic-and-basement palace stood just as firmly as it did in 1957, built from square brick by solid, working-class Italian contractors. The house had stood up against rain, sleet, wind, hail, and a thousand more caustic elements. Graffiti never stuck to it, whether it was painted on by the Panthers, the Skinheads, or the Muslim Brotherhood. It was a Black "All In the Family" custom factory-made special, if there ever was one.

Catherine Williams gave birth to five children within those walls. Everything else she needed was within an eight-block radius. Why venture across town where the Chinese steamed their rice, the East Indians burned their incense, and the Jamaicans smoked their weed? The prices in the all-white burbs were twice as high, the products were half as good, the selection generic as the Donny Osmond and Don Johnson wannabes who shopped there.

Catherine spent a lifetime complaining about the neighborhood she loved so much. TV would tell her what lies the world wanted her to believe. Nathan's phone calls would tell her the truth.

She hadn't stepped outside the house since she had gotten the news about Nathan's death. It was Nathan who called home only three times a year, and maybe sent a card. It was Nathan who always seemed to be on the most-wanted lists of the Feds and the Street Lords. But it was Nathan whom Catherine waited for and loved most.

Catherine didn't cash the settlement check from the transport company, whose vehicle inadvertently caused the accident that killed

Nathan. Perhaps it was a gesture of defiance. Perhaps it was another black, middle-aged male underneath the wreckage.

Ross rang again. Still no answer, no footsteps.

"Maybe she's not home," Leona said desperately.

"She's in there. And so's what we came for," Ross repeated, with the determination of a first-rate horse trainer tossed off a spoiled two-year-old gelding who still imagined himself a stallion.

Leona peeked into the window. There it was Nathan's "good luck" box. It stood in the middle of an old oak table, unopened. "It's eerie. This house looks like it's built around that 'box'. It looks like a monument, or a coffin," she commented.

"Or a good luck shrine. Something that has the answer to your hardest questions." Ross's eyes glossed over, overtaken with a mystical presence he experienced in the Apache and Hopi high country.

"Nathan's mother is upstairs, chained to her bed and a bottle of bourbon, or she's not here. We have to break in."

"That would be illegal." Ross rang the bell again.

"Ross. That box has information that could help me find my brother, help you save 'President Kennedy', and, if all of this is true, put away more shitheads and assholes than the Velochi papers or even Watergate. It makes sense to go in there and take it."

"Sometimes you have to do what doesn't make sense."

Ross knocked. Leona screamed. Her cries of desperation were rewarded.

From inside, the flush of a toilet. Then, footsteps. Then, a screeching voice, more like a shrill from the other side of the grave. "I'm coming, I'm coming."

"And I'm leaving," Leona said under her breath. Ross grabbed her by the collar and pulled her back to the door. "What are you doing?"

"Keeping a good, green horse on a narrow trail, so it doesn't fall down a big cliff."

"Screw you. Go to hell, Ross," Leona grunted through a fake smile, as Catherine opened the first of five bolt-locks. "Go to hell."

"I'm already there, darling. So are you." Ross sucked in his gut, ready for the emotional bullride of his life.

Catherine Williams stood a towering five-feet nothing, most of her 140 pounds in the most unattractive places. The gray Brillo pad on her head was more kink than hair, and she squinted behind glasses half an inch thick. There was something intense about the woman, something very cutting-edge. She knew the score and refused to play the game. Maybe that was why she was, despite her efforts, a feisty 72-year-old going on 25.

"Who are you?" Catherine blasted out, fire in her eyes, thunder in her voice, a sawed-off shotgun locked under her armpit.

"Friends of Nathanial, ma'am. From New Mexico," Ross said.

Catherine eyed Ross up and down, looking for any proof to the contrary. On first glance, he passed. But Leona didn't.

"And who are you?" Catherine blasted out in a soft voice.

"Also a friend of Nate," the reply. "From Arizona."

Catherine thought a second, looked into Leona's soul through her blank stare, then raised her shotgun barrel. "Nathanial didn't have any friends in Arizona who talked like you. And he didn't have any friends who called him Nate. You two sell your Gospel sermons, vacuum cleaners, or whatever else you've got somewhere else. You step any closer, I'd be obligated to shoot you as trespassers."

Leona's eye glanced toward the box.

"What are you looking at, dead woman!!!" Catherine yelled out, her threat made all the more real by the barrel of the gun firmly inserted under Leona's quivering neck. "What the hell are you looking at!!!"

"The box that holds Excalibre," Ross calmly stated. He gave her a sympathy card, a very personal note inside it.

Catherine grabbed Leona, holding her against the wall with a cold, steel barrel ready to fire. But the card was real, as was the reference.

"What do you know about 'Excalibre', Mormon man?" Catherine demanded.

"Do I look like a Mormon?"

"You look like someone who knows more about my son than anyone else who came by. They were a lot more clever than you, too. Offered me all kinds of money, travel vacations, and a new house, too. But I took care of this neighborhood, and it takes care of me. None of those Mormon bastards made it out of here. Not alive, anyway. Black bullets put them white fuckers in brown body bags. This Whitebread Mormon bitch will fit fine in a brown body bag. Just one phone call is all I gotta make, and...."

"Professor Jack. Have you heard from Professor Jack, ma'am?" Ross interrupted.

"You know Professor Jack, Mormon man?"

"I know that saving Professor Jack, and being sure that Nathanial didn't die for nothing, depends on me opening that box."

Catherine stared at the styrofoam-cardboard box. "I didn't open it. The good lock is still in it. No one is supposed to open it."

"Until Nathanial is in a better place," Leona interrupted. "He was a good person. He has to be in a better place now, right?"

Catherine hesitated, but still kept her guests at gunpoint. They said all the right words. They had to know what was in Nathan's heart; they had to be his friends, or maybe they were his worst enemies, hanging around like vultures, waiting to eat the last, most valuable part of him.

"What's in the box?" Leona asked.

"If you were so close to 'Nate', you should know," Catherine countered. "Were you the one who sent Nathanial's good luck box to me?"

"Yes," Ross interjected. "Unopened. The way he wanted it sent. Till Nathanial is home, or in a better place, his box is home. His soul is in a better place."

"And you want me to open it?"

"Yes." Ross held firm.

"Did Nathaniel ask you to open it?"

"No."

"And you want me to trust you. With my son's most precious possession. His luck."

"Yes." Catherine thought. With the gun down, she used her most effective weapon her penetrating stare. She opened fire on Ross first.

"You don't look like a Mormon. But you look honest. Right now, that's enough."

Catherine moved on to Leona. She trembled so much that she froze, rigid in body, mind, and spirit.

"You, Mormon lady. You don't believe in anything at all. Not God, not the Church, not even in yourself. What the eggheads call a cynic. You look naked. Terrified, but you do what you have to do, anyway. You must have been one of Nathan's best friends."

"I was," Leona said, eyes down. "For a little while," she continued, looking straight into Catherine's eyes. Leona remembered small moments, brief times. The time between the motel room door closing and the end of the contractual lay, when she was sent to extract information about the Professor, after one of the many times Nathan had left the "Last Chance Cafe" for the last time. The time when he stopped to help her on the road, for the brief moment when she thought that Hardball really DID abandon her on a cold, desolate desert road with an empty tank of gas, no money, and a paper-thin leather-fringed coat.

Catherine knew that Leona was hiding more lies and that she was new to telling the truth. It made no sense to trust her. Of all the people who came to find out what Nathan was about, or wanted to be about, she showed the most contradictions. A person living on both sides of the fence. Just one more question to ask.

"What's your name?" Catherine asked, demanding an honest answer.

"Leona?"

"That's a question, honey. You don't answer questions with questions. What is your name?"

"Leona."

"Leona, what?"

Leona hesitated. Time to be pragmatic, practical, and to use her brain, perhaps for the first time in years. "Leona Diamantis."

"Related to Hardball Harold Diamantis?" Catherine reached for the gun.

One final answer would end all the guilt, the pain, the misery.

"He was my father," Leona related, and confessed.

"So the bastard's dead?"

"No, I am," Leona answered.

Catherine's suspicions were right, after all. Leona was more than a whore made up to look respectable. But though she had a conscience, she still had a secret. Catherine pressed on, determined to get to the truth no matter what the consequences. "Did Hardball Harold kill my Nathanial?"

Leona opened her mouth, praying that the right words would come out. "No," Ross interjected. "Hardball Harold watched. Someone else killed Nathanial."

"Who?" Catherine demanded.

"Someone who is dead now. We both killed her," Ross said, with affirmation and authority of feeling.

Leona fell into a sheltered emotional zone so new that she felt frightened.

"So," Ross asked. "Can we look in the box?"

Catherine laid down her weapon. "You had the courage to come in here. To walk out on Hardball Harold. Blood's blood, but the truth's stronger than blood. Nathanial believed that. And you killed the bitch who killed my Nathanial. You deserve some of his luck."

"Thank you," Ross replied. With that, he opened the box and looked inside. He photographed what he had to, and remembered the rest. Names, numbers, and events put the Marcello and the Illuminati in the middle of most current crises that have plagued the world since World War II. The archaeological dig was an 'X-File' sunken treasure pot, as long as there was a Mulder and Scully to bring it all to the surface. "This IS the real box, right?" Ross asked. "You could have put Nathan's 'luck' into another box, put bad luck, or wrong information, into this one."

"Yeah. I could have," Catherine replied, with her best poker face.

As a recreational gambler, Ross could see through a bluff, but only if his life didn't depend on it. He did his best to pretend that the hand didn't matter, though he knew it was the most important game he had ever played. But Catherine was sincere. He remembered the New York credo, "Sincerity is the most powerful weapon you've got and if you can fake that…"

Leona watched through a flood of tears. Catherine gave her comfort, tea, and a change of emotional perspective; a fair exchange, all around.

CHAPTER 34

The "Western Standard Motel" lived up to its name. Standard-rates. Standard-sized parking spots. Standard rules regarding pets and after-hours noise. Fitting for a standard registration.

"How long will you be staying, Mister Smith?" the clerk asked.

"Long enough for me and my wife, Mary, to get some rest, then be back on the road to Omaha," Ross replied.

"We only have one room left. With a single bed, a small one at that," the clerk replied.

"We'll take it," Leona spouted out.

At last, some response, Ross thought to himself. Leona hadn't spouted out a smart-assed insult to Ross, or a cynical dig at life, since leaving the Williams' house three hundred miles ago. He baited her at every turn. Even the "John and Mary Smith" didn't get a rise out of her.

"Mary is interested in what kind of nightlife you have here. She needs a night out."

"No, she doesn't," Leona blasted out from under her blonde wig and bug-eyed sunglasses.

The clerk smiled. "The room has cable TV, radio, and a couch, in case you need some extra space."

Leona kept her emotions hidden, buried under a solemn silence. It was the kind of silence that allowed guilt to grow, the kind of grief that women seemed to hold on to far longer than men. Leona was very much the woman. She would hold on to her grief until it destroyed her. It was the least she could do.

"We just want to reset our brains, then move on to some important business," Ross appended, after treating himself to a fabricated history on the register information card. It felt like a moral shopping spree for a man who spent ten years sitting on a fortune and not spending a penny of it. "We have family affairs that have to be corrected. Right, Mary?" he continued.

"Sure, 'John'," Leona reply.

At least it was something, Ross thought. A start. Leona would have to use her aggression against very powerful enemies, not against herself. Her depression was so deep that verbal reminders like "your brother's life depends on how assertively you can fight the Illuminati" floated over her bowed head and glazed eyes.

Upon entry into the room, Leona locked the door behind her, then closed the shades. "We're still hiding from Hardball Harold, right?" she said.

"We're attacking him, and his organization," Ross reply. He unpacked his suitcase, finding himself wondering what it would be like to be one of the "normal" people, but knowing that he was never really one of them, and never could be. He turned on the tube, Monday Night Football, Denver vs. Dallas.

Leona could see the sparkle in Ross's eyes as a five-foot-ten Denver Bronco halfback broke through the invincible defensive line of America's team. Dallas was beatable, as long as the little guy ran fast enough and hard enough. History was being made here. The 1 and 8 Broncos were on the verge of whipping the Dallas Cowboys and ruining their chances of getting into the playoffs. Insignificant matters such as finding Professor Jack, Harry, and foiling the Illuminati-Diamantis empire would have to wait.

Ross found himself cheering with the Denver hometown crowd. Millions of other Bronco fans were doing the same. Finally, Ross was on the same side as his fellow New Mexican's and Arizonan's on a clear-cut, all-or-none, winner-take-all issue that everyone could understand.

Leona looked in the full-length mirror. With a mixture of courage and curiosity, she took off her sunglasses, then the blonde wig. She looked into eyes she hardly recognized. "I feel . . . destructive, Ross. What am I supposed to do about that?"

"Ride it out," he said sincerely, out of the side of his mouth. "The closer you are to life, the more you feel the magnet of death."

"Why?"

"Don't know. It's just like that. The more destructive you feel, the closer you are to life. The important thing is to use the better side of your brain. The smarter side of your head. The more connected side of your soul."

"Sounds profound. What happens if you can't tell up from down?"

"Then you just keep on going till you can, Leona." Ross's connection to the Infinite Wisdom was blissfully interrupted by an onside Denver kick, which the Broncos turned into a touchdown. "Whooooo!!!!!" he screamed out, with a yelp loud enough to blow a hole into the eardrums of every arrogant Texan banker and lawyer in Dallas.

Leona felt herself smiling. At least Ross knew one way to connect to life. But did she? "I'm gonna take a shower. Wash off all this . . . grunge."

"Sure, Babe."

Maybe the term of endearment was a slip. Maybe a reflex reactivated from the Monday Night Football nights in the earlier blissful years of Ross's marriage. Or maybe it was real.

Leona looked one more time at the sweat caking into the newly-formed wrinkles on her face, the dirt-stained tattoos on her thigh, and her long, brown mane, which was more grease than hair.

The view from the bathroom mirror was more dangerous. More light, more mirror, and more isolation from the world. She came in well-prepared for action. Sharp edges would be required, with decisive action.

"The closer you feel to death, the more connected you are to life, right?" she said to herself. She reached inside Ross's shaving kit. She took the scissors into her trembling hand. The blades were shiny, newly sharpened.

"Change your hair, change your life, right?" she said to herself as she grabbed her three-foot mane, the topknot she swore she would never surrender to fads, casting agents, lovers, or even her father. Now she prepared herself to surrender it to her worst enemy, self-sabotage.

The first cut took off two feet from the front, at the level of the nose. The sight of four years of growth on the floor felt liberating and frightening. But, more than anything, it was an isolating experience. Isolation from life is what she sought, and a Sinead O'Connor- Yul Brenner makeover would do it.

A second cut took off a mound from the back, done just below the neck. The point of no return. No stylist in the world could convert her into a long-haired, brown-eyed Woodstock beauty now. She grabbed the left half of her mane, closed her eyes, and then prepared to make the decisive cut, just above the ears. She closed her eyes, winced, then screamed.

Ross rushed in, grabbing the scissors from her hand.

"What the hell are you doing?" Ross screamed out, trying to prevent her from finishing the job.

"I'm tired of being me. I wanna be someone else. I wanna be someone else," Leona screeched out like a hawk after prey, then like a mouse about to be eaten. "I wanna be someone else."

"You are somebody else. And you're gonna be someone better and happier than you are now, as long as you…"

"As long as I do what, 'Cowboy Ross'? As long as I what?"

"I don't know. I don't know."

"And who am I supposed to change with? Who for?"

"For yourself."

"Bullshit, Ross."

"Then for your brother, Harry."

"Harry's probably dead."

"Then for the world."

"The world doesn't give a shit about me."

"But I do." The words slipped out of Ross's mouth. No marriage proposal was more profound, and simply put.

"Okay, 'Cowboy Ross.' You like me so much, you make me into someone else. Anything you want me to be."

Leona offered Ross the abundance of her jagged, shoulder-length brown mane, then rammed the scissors into his trembling hand.

"This isn't a good idea, Leona. You have a part of you that destroys yourself, I have a part of me that destroyed."

"Others? Come on, Ross. You shape me in your image, or I'll shape me in mine. And I guarantee that you are not going to like it."

"We can go to a professional."

"Bullshit, Ross. Why don't you do it?"

"I might go too far. Cut it off at the roots, or below it. Or worse."

"Maybe you will. I'm willing to take that chance. Are you?"

"I don't know." Ross felt himself on the fence, remembering the days when it was so easy to lash out at his destructive urges toward others.

"You feel close to death, Ross? So do I. That means we're both close to life. Blissfully in, what do you call it, love?"

Ross looked into Leona's eyes through the mirror. He felt his hands rising, his brain thinking again. An image was forming in his head, but could he trust it? Would he dare to inflict it on Leona?

"Go ahead, Ross. I trust you. I'm probably the only one who really does."

Ross grabbed Leona's mane, moved the scissors toward the roots of her hair, then moved his hands back. His hands framed a pristine image too frightening to bring into the world of forms.

"Your daughter, the one in the pictures who never comes home," Leona said. "I still have enough to look like your daughter. Bangs, wings just below the ears. With a little tail down the neck that you can twirl around your finger. Cute. Perky. Blonde? Just like when she was fifteen."

Ross hesitated. Guilt overtook his eyes.

"I was sick. I'm not going to do to you what I did to her."

"I'm asking you. As an adult. And a friend."

"You're sure."

"I'm sure, Ross."

"I wish I were."

"Love is about taking chances, not about being sure, Ross. So I'm told."

With that, Ross conferred her rite of passage with the first cut, his rite of passage with the second. The rest led the pair of fugitives into a world of their own that took them into carnal bliss, then the first restful sleep Ross and Leona shared with anyone. The night seemed to last forever. Only one problem remained in the wings; the next morning.

CHAPTER 35

"The price of enlightenment is insanity, the cost of knowing the truth is being alone, the albatross of being alive is being constantly restless and unheard amongst the walking dead." The improvised dialogue came out of Harry's mouth during the second take, like fire out of the mouth of a dragon. A whole layer of depth found its way into "Code to Die For." A depth so intense and so insightful that even Professor Jack hadn't envisioned it.

"I just got one question," Harry asked after David yelled "cut," the scene having been shot to well beyond the level of anyone's expectations. "What the hell is an albatross?"

"A cross to bear. A man's gotta do what a man's gotta do. All that crap," Associate Producer Carole Steinberg related. "Why?"

"I don't know," Harry confessed, while preparing for the next shot, sweat pouring down his face on the only day L.A. had snow in the last three years. "I just think that I should, like, know where I've been flying to, maybe even while I'm there."

"Is that what it feels like? Flying?" Carole pressed on. Maybe she could forge Harry's newfound relation to the Formless Infinite with a standard story structure relatable to 15-year-old airheads in training to be structural engineers, 16-year-old mothers trying to be women, or other operators of the global multinational company otherwise referred to as "society."

"Yeah," Harry replied. "Flying. I don't know where I'm headed, but I feel like I'm burning up. Like I can't stop till I crash, and that if I keep this insanity alive in me, I will…" He stopped, unable to verbalize the word.

"You'll what?" David asked.

"Finish the best movie ever made," Carole interjected. "And maybe even under budget. This might be the first one of Davy's movies where the star gets more credit than the director. The credits should read, a film by Rex. We can always arrange it in post-production."

"The hell you will!" David yelled back as the crew took a step away, anticipating a blow-up that would measure a full ten on the Richter scale this time. The Entertainment Tonight cameras and tabloid gossip mongers moved in for a closer look.

"Look," Carole blasted at David through a pasty L.A. all-is-great smile. "It's a marketing thing. All of this is a marketing thing. Anyone who's passionate about media is a moron, a fool, or…."

"A visionary?" David interjected.

"Rex is a visionary, maybe. But you, Davy. You weren't born to it. Neither was I. All of this is negotiable. Rex has been rewriting every scene, anyway."

"Yeah. Changing all the facts, but still keeping everything about the way things REALLY work very accurate. Even truthful."

"Impressive, David. Why are you so philosophical? Usually, it happens to people who are ready to die."

Carole had hit the nail right on the head, and David felt the hammer's blow. She went in for the kill.

"You HAVE been talking to your silent partner, David. And the investment board we never tell the cameras about. Have you been made 'expendable'?"

"I can still bring you down. And I still control this movie. If this movie is done my way, it'll bring in all the money, clout, and power I need."

"And if it's done Rex's way?"

David hesitated. "I don't know. He's got a very hidden agenda. You can't get to it, I can't get to it, and I can't get him interested enough in any hooker to tell her what he's all about."

"So he IS gay."

"No, he's not."

"Maybe he's infatuated with YOU, Davy boy." She pursed her lips mockingly.

"No. He's in love with someone else. A very Platonic relationship. Maybe even a spiritual one. That's gotta be the reason why he's doing 'Code to Die For'. No one can be so passionate without being driven by, or for, someone else." For the first time in a long while, David felt an emotion he could not handle; sincerity.

Carole rewarded him with mock applause.

"If you were a guy, I'd deck you," David grunted out.

"Maybe I am."

"No, Carole. You're a power bitch running on empty, to a dead end you've already hit. You have nothing to say, so you keep trying to upgrade the window-dressing. You live alone, work alone, and will die alone."

Carole turned silent. "Touché," she wanted to say, but couldn't. Hit by the truth in a painful place, she struck back. "You have been converted, David."

"By what?" David asked.

"Whatever insanity is driving Rex into stardom, then into the grave."

David took a look down the studio lot. It had happened already. The magnificent flight had ended in a big crash. No survivors.

Harry had made the biggest mistake of his new life as a spiritual aviator, he shut the engines off. He had taken a five-minute nap after a sleep deprivation marathon. The catnap led to deep sleep, thanks to the skilled and loving hands of Naomi, a 20-year-old supermodel wannabe who could barely read the inside cover of a fashion magazine. The snooze lasted only ten minutes, but that was enough time for Harry to fall from the heavens.

"I can't do it. I won't do it. I don't have to do it." Harry repeated to himself.

"You HAVE to do it," David reminded him.

"Why?" Harry's eyes sincerely asked for an answer, and nothing would do but the truth this time. "Why do I have to do it?"

"I don't know." David looked downward. The crew looked at him with bewilderment. The First Assistant Director looked at his watch. Not another director-actor problem he would have to deal with. Then again, it would not be the first time an Assistant Director got a field promotion after the Captain shot himself in the foot in the heat of battle. The ultimate boss was the studio, their boss the Illuminati. "Code to Die" had to get made, or a lot of people would look bad.

Then there was Hardball Harold, never present but always there. His ghost hung over David and Harry, Jr. like an apparition with a loaded .45 Colt, ready to fire if even a wrong idea was thought.

"Hardball will find me here," Harry let spill out of his tired lips. "Besides, Jack IS crazy, right?"

"Right," David said. His victory had been won, his suspicions confirmed. Rex was indeed the prodigal son whom Hardball wanted dead. The invisible protector of the elusive "Professor Jack" had finally been apprehended.

But David couldn't collect his well-earned bounty. He found himself admiring the young outlaw in Harry, and even worshipping the old sage in Professor Jack. Maybe it was the script, the energy, or the madness of the creative process finally catching up with him.

"What are we gonna do?" Harry asked, seeking in David's eyes advice, as well as friendship.

"Today, make a movie."

"And tomorrow?"

"Become one?"

"My real name is Harry. What's yours?"

David hesitated. "Norman. Norman Reinseelhouf." The mystery name he kept under wraps for so long finally came out.

"Being a 'Norman' pretending to be a 'David' isn't as bad as being a 'Harry' trying to be a . . . who am I supposed to be?"

"Rex."

Harry smiled. His death would be a comfortable one. Finally, he gave up control to those who were in control. It felt safe, and Harry hadn't felt safe for a long time.

"You know, Norman. I didn't surrender. I just made a settlement. I wasn't supposed to go crazy. That wasn't part of the deal. I just wanna be normal. You ever just wanna be normal, Norman?"

"Yeah. Normal isn't so bad." David tried the thought on for size, not knowing if it really fit. He gave a thumbs up to the crew, publicity cameras, and then to Carole. There was still enough residual fire in Harry to finish principal photography. Today, Davy boy would make a movie. Tomorrow, David would turn in the one who, perhaps, was the only friend he ever really had.

CHAPTER 36

"Hey!!!" Hardball Harold screamed at the new man at his old pizza joint on Morris Park Avenue. "I wanted a slice, with extra cheese, onions, pepperoni, and olives. This slab of shit looks like it was made in Iowa. What is this?"

"Ham and pineapple, with raisins," the clerk said, his face straight out of a Norman Rockwell painting, his accent pure Generic Mid-America. "You did order the Hawaiian Special." He pointed at a laminated menu, standard issue for the New Josepi Pizzeria chain.

"Cute. You got the "p" word in there."

"The what, Sir?"

"'P' for pasta. You Yuppie queers can tell the difference between twenty kinds of coffee beans, but it's too much work for you to remember the difference between rigatoni, spaghetti, linguini, and spaghettini."

"Spaghettini, Sir?"

"Small strand of spaghetti. About the size of your dick. Right, guys?" He turned around, retesting his ability to sign on new recruits to his city-wide army of soldiers and sympathizers.

The old farts who came in for old-fashioned Josepi Pizzeria smiled. The young shitheads backed away. The over-thirty women got offended. The younger ones edged in, eager to see who would win.

An undercover cop unbuckled the holster of his gun and lined himself up to get a clear shot out, if required to. Rick Manelli wanted to make it into the big time. Whether it would be by protecting Hardball Harry or gunning him down, it didn't matter. Manelli ate enough shit in the Academy during his years as a traffic control officer. He was not going to settle for anything less than a six-figure income or a seven-figure reputation.

The clerk continued. "Sir, I can . . ."

"Look," Hardball Harold interrupted. "I'm not a 'sir'. My name is Harold Diamantis. You know what that means?"

"That I should call you Mister Diamantis?" the clerk countered.

"Look, Gomer. Make you a deal. Negotiate a price for a real slice."

"A slice is two dollars. Standard chain price policy, Sir."

"Nothing's standard price."

Harold took off his watch, cufflinks, tie clasp, and ring. He laid them on the table. "Make you a proposition, Gomer. All of this is yours. The watch is worth more than you earn in six months. The tie clasp will go real good with the big selection of clip-ons you bought at Disney World. And the ring is a twenty-carat fuckin' diamond. Bright enough to blind you if the light is just right, and sharp enough to cut a jugular vein. That's the big blood vessel in the neck, Gomer."

Hardball grabbed Manelli, demonstrating the location of the vein. A pool of urine poured down Manelli's trouser leg.

Hardball whipped out a crisp hundred-dollar bill. "Here, buy yourself another pair of trousers." Harold pulled out Manelli's badge, displaying it to everyone in the room. "And get yourself another occupation."

Harold called in the hookers from outside the window. "Look, girls. The most famous undercover cop in New York. I'm giving him another hundred. You take him down and get your picture taken with him for the cover of Screw magazine." He turned around to Manelli. "And if these kids in here wanna smoke a little weed to ease the tension, what's the dif, right?"

Harold tossed the career-climbing cop out on the pavement. Manelli's elbow hit the bricks hard; his shield hit even harder. "Hey, Manelli. It's nothing personal. Assholes like your father got me tossed out of the force, so I take it out on assholes like you. You can take it out on younger assholes when you get to be a man. It's the way it works."

The hookers laughed, grateful to have been spared another arrest. Manelli ran like a scared rabbit, all the way back to his upstate hometown. Harold felt hungry for a slice of traditional pizza in his old neighborhood hangout.

One of the kids inside The New Josepi's smiled. "Look, Hardball said. "I feel generous today. Your friend over there has the dope, you share it with each other. Even value. No price gouging."

Hardball carved new items into the laminated menu, "Weed, fifty bucks an ounce; Crack, a hundred a snort; new drinking age.."

"is still twenty-one, Sir," the clerk interrupted. In his shaking hand, a revolver. In his eyes, intense fear at the thought of having to use it.

"Gomer. I'm damn impressed with you," Harry said. "Bet you're impressed with yourself, too."

"John, my name's John," the clerk replied. "And I'm paid to keep this establishment open, operating, and safe for clientele."

"Well, John. Maybe we should start over. I'm still hungry. Hungry as all shit for a real Josepi slice. I'm gonna fuckin' die unless I get one. And I have a thousand bucks."

Harold waved up the money like a red flag. John lowered his gun.

"The price is two dollars."

"For the crap you make. I wanna pay you, Gomer-now-John, a thousand bucks for a slice of real Josepi pizza."

"Sounds like I'd be ripping you off, Mister Diamantis."

"Maybe. But you have a product. Real stuff. Dough, parmesan, mozzarella, olive oil. Ovens. Real food that people eat and need. All I got is ten pieces of fuckin' green paper. Can't eat green paper, enjoy its aroma, use it to keep your body fuckin' alive."

"And your point, Mister Diamatis?"

"A question that's been bothering me for a long time," Harold paced around John like a lion, edging into, but never penetrating into, the farmboy's personal zone.

"What's your question, Mister Diamantis?"

"Who's more important to a deal? Who calls the shots? Who makes the rules? The guy with the product, the real stuff people want, need, and can use? Or the guy who has the money?"

"Money talks, everybody else walks. The paying customer is always right. Correct, Mister Diamantis?"

"John-boy. You don't believe that crap. If you did, you wouldn't have had the courage to stick a gun in my face. The commitment to put your fuckin' ass on the line for a room full of people you don't know from a fuckin' cockroach."

"Then the person with the power is the person with the product, not the money?"

"Right, John. But you gotta say it like a statement, not a question."

"The person with the power is the person with the product."

"Or the gun," Harold interrupted. He grabbed John's revolver, pushed him against the wall, and emptied the chamber into his head.

John's body slid across the floor, leaving in its wake a trail of blood. Harold sampled it with his finger.

"Tastes better than the fuckin' tomato sauce you were putting on the slice you tried to sell me . . . And all these good people in here."

The crowd froze, their emotions paralyzed. Gen-Xers, babyboomers, and Roosevelt generation offspring were all united by one common experience, terror.

"A tragic suicide. So tragic," Hardball commented as he carved out John's liver, then sprinkled it on an unbaked pizza. He put it in the oven.

"We're all gonna have lunch together. Johnboy, here, was more worthy of living than any of you. But I had to kill him. Ain't my rule.

But maybe if you eat some of his liver, you might get some of his guts. Johnboy reminds me of my own kid, and what's gotta become of HIM."

Harold distributed the slices of liver pizza all around. He ensured that everyone partook.

"And now, something from you. Any piece of picture identification. This way, I got something on all of you, one way or the other. Or I can find something. Just in case any of you decide to become noble."

Hardball gathered his belongings, pocketed the I.D.s of his luncheon guests, holstered John's gun, and calmly walked toward the door. "Whoever barfs up, cleans it up. I'm going to see a movie."

Harold was smart enough not to let on that the "Code to Die For" set was his next stop. If all went according to plan, the next station on his express train to the top would be the top a seat on the Illuminati High Council. From there, he could rule the world from the top, as well as the bottom.

CHAPTER 37

"Remember, 'Rex'. The final day of shooting's the hardest," David related to Harry, as the makeup artist put the last layer of plastic blood over his eyelids.

"Does everyone forget their lines? Ask the foreman for their checks?" Harry asked.

"They bring all their egos, grudges, and problems on set. All those contracts of creative co-operation go out the window, and the whole fuckin' place blows up. Yelling, screaming, and throwing iron bars. Once I saw the wife of the most macho man in L.A. draw a gun on her ex-husband, and co-star."

"What happened?"

"He killed her in the tabloids. Then she hired a real hit man to arrange an accident for him on his motorcycle trip through Baja."

"Where the hell is Baja, David?"

"California . . . Harry."

Harry looked at his face in the makeup room mirror. More blood, pus, and bone than flesh, it did make him look like he had been through hell. He hardly recognized himself. Even the groupie P.A.s passed him by like he was just another $75 a day extra. "I'm glad we're shooting this in sequence. And in New York. Home town . . . This IS the last scene, right, David?"

"Right, Harry," the reply. No look could have said 'Judas' more deeply. David knew it would be the last scene of much more than just a movie. So did Harry.

"The private investor we never talked about, David. Mister D. Is he coming on set?"

"Yeah. But he hasn't seen the dailies. No one outside our creative staff has. We're gonna keep the footage away from the press and the investors as long as possible. A publicity thing."

"And a survival thing?"

David hesitated. "That's a very prophetic answer, Harry."

"What the hell does 'prophetic' mean?"

"It means that you're very right about a lot of things. A lot more right than you know you are."

"And want to be," Harry added. "I just have one request."

"What?"

"We do it in one take. For real. With the script that I wrote last night. No changes."

David scanned through the script, whipping through it too fast to read it, but with enough time to see what he was afraid to.

"Harry. You can't use these names or these things they did. We can change them."

"No, we can't."

"The audience will get the idea. A big mega-trillion-dollar organization in control of the world gets blackmailed by the little guy, then gets destroyed. It's the idea people want to see."

"But it's the reality that they have to see." Harry stood his ground. The fire surged into his eyes for one more fight with the inevitable foe, an opponent who had him marked for death since the day of his birth.

"Okay. Everybody out. That means everybody." David commanded, and the cast and crew shuffled out, dragging their tired feet. "Come on, DeNiro and Scorsese are outside and want your autographs."

A dark silence fell over the trailer, made all the more ominous by the morning sun penetrating its rays through the venetian blinds.

"Look, Harry. I can get you out of here before a certain relation of yours finds out about your new movie career. Hardball doesn't have to know anything. I can even have him retire from the business and life. But you have to give me something."

"My ten million dollar paycheck, David?"

"Pocket change, Harry."

"My friendship?"

"Worthless currency once the bullets start flying."

"The knowledge that you did something that makes a difference."

"NO one makes a difference, Harry. The chips just keep changing hands in a very small room. Ninety-nine percent of the wealth, power, and fun belong to one percent of the people. Everyone's okay with that arrangement. Even the ninety-nine percent of the world who are schleps. They like being schleps. You used to be one, remember?"

Harry remembered the three lifetimes of changes he had undergone since he met the crazy eccentric in the New Mexican desert. Though he desperately wanted to go back to being "normal," even "miserable," there was no way he could now.

"The names and criminal offenses stay on, David. Not yours, but all the others. It's time the Illuminati board members get full credit for their work."

"How the hell did you get the list? That old lunatic from New Mexico you've been hanging with?"

"And your computer. And some other places. Your girlfriends talk a lot. So do you, in your sleep, 'Davy'. I name them, not you. You get in, take over the Illuminati, give the world back to the schleps you stole it from, then dissolve the Illuminati, and anything else like it. If you keep it going, he-we-dissolve you."

David felt a chill through his whole body. "Water. I need a glass of . . . Fuck this, I need something stronger."

David pulled out a stunt gun, pointing it at Harry.

"Does that have any bullets in it?"

"It might. And I am prepared to use it."

"Then I suggest that you do, David. But the names and events are already in the dailies. Hidden between the words. I snuck into the editing room and dubbed them in myself. I even made a non-director's rough cut of the flick. Even put in my own music. I don't suck too much on the harp or slide guitar."

"How, Harry?"

"When you guys were partying, I put your studio to some alternative use. Hundred-year-old scotch can buy any security guard. Great dope can make any editor do exactly what you want, and more."

"We know where the lab sends the footage. And we control ALL the distributors."

"Bet they're not the distributors who are on MY list. And the press does have an advance copy of the script. Press can always beat politicos."

"Then they... we... will take away their ink, paper, and TV cameras."

"But somewhere, somehow, the truth is going to come out. How they-you-fuckers controlled the stock market and currency exchange. How you start, then profit from, small-change wars in places like Vietnam, Nicaragua, Bosnia, and the Middle East. And in case all else fails, you hit democracy where it lives; the voting booth. No election in history has turned out the way you wanted it to. But you guys were real stupid when you fixed the Quebec separation vote thing up in Canada. 50.1% for Quebec staying with Canada, 49.9% for separating. Canada still stays a country divided against itself. Ontario remains the biggest trading partner the United States has. And the American colony of Canada still gets to export all its natural resources to American Industry, so Illuminati-owned and operated manufacturers can sell products back to the Canucks at a 1500 percent markup. Then, for fun, you have Presidents killed when . . ."

"That was Carlos Marcello's idea," David interrupted.

"And your muscle."

"their muscle, Harry. I wasn't even BORN when Kennedy got shot in 1963."

"Neither was I."

"'Professor Jack' is gonna bring you down on this one. He's gonna bring all of us down. Besides, Harry, do you really know that he's JFK? He has his doubts about it himself."

Harry hesitated, halted by self-doubt. David lost no time in using that Achilles heel of every noble warrior.

"Look, Harry. What's in it for you if you pass up a billion-dollar career in movies? I'm offering you a chance to get paid for expressing exactly what you feel. Do you know how many, many people in this country have to make a living by NOT expressing what they feel inside them?"

"Yeah," Harry countered, staring into David's face. "I'm looking at one of them right now."

The inevitable knock on the door came from the first Assistant Director. "David. We're ready to shoot. Everyone's ready, and waiting." David and Harry peeked out of the trailer window. The heralder was right, maybe even prophetic.

Comfortably seated behind the camera, Hardball Harry, in sunglasses, a cheesy wide-lapel suit jacket, and a million-dollar all-will-be-well smile. Behind him, an escort guard, with more firepower under their jackets than the entire studio-hired security staff combined. Lining the police barricade, a wall of "schleps", pushing each other into the pavement for a view of the biggest drama of the decade. In the loneliest bleacher seat on the highest roof, Professor Jack, armed with a surveillance mike, a handful of forty-five caliber bullets, and the determination to put right what thirty years had made very, very wrong.

CHAPTER 38

Professor Jack knew that the only difference between a watchdog and a sniper is that a sniper had to be his own master.

He had three enemies. The Illuminati-paired goons on the 'Code the Die For' movie set below had a hundred rounds for each of Jack's. All that would be required for them to open fire up into the roof, or into their star wonderboy "Rex", would be a grunt from Hardball Harry, a grin from David, or a nod of a finger from one of the Illuminati high board members who had to be amongst the crowd, somewhere. They were Jack's real enemies. They ordered Carlos Marcello's "assassination" plan to be carried through in 1963, by unanimous vote. So the letter of confession, written on a secret deathbed, was read.

Jack carried the letter with him always, entrusting it to no one. Not Nathan, not even Harry. It took too much courage for Lee Osterberg to write the letter, and it was sent with the request that it remain confidential.

Lee still had family, somewhere. Jack thought it best not to have his name mentioned in the script. Whether out of compassion or honor in the heat of battle, he was never sure. But a man's last request had to be honored, even if it was a former Illuminati board member, the lowest form of man, or woman, possible.

A black cloud came over the set, abruptly covering the bright sun. "You bastard!" Director of Photography Lance Irwin yelled up to the sky. The bronzed Californian summa cum laude UCLA film school grad had a God-given eye for knowing how to make every shot look great. His very visual eye won him three Oscars, but he still had a grade 5 reading ability.

Lance wouldn't tolerate anything that could ruin the composition of a great shot, most especially rain clouds from Mother Nature. "That's it, you sadistic, dried-up old Bitch!!! Do you have any fucking idea how much time it's gonna take to relight this set? Why the fuck don't you fuck one of the other gods, or goddesses? We have a human lesbo from the set. We've got fag hags. Girly-boys. Girly-men. You can have your fuckin' pick of pathetic, human sacrifices. I deserve some good fucking lighting, and no goddamn rain!!!"

"We'll fix it in post," David interjected as he walked onto the main shooting area with Harry. "We have a new thing called 'editing' that can make a dark day look bright," he said out of the side of his mouth, as he gave a big L.A. "all is well" smile to the New York-based ENG reporters.

The wind contributed its commentary. Just as Lance was about to give the finger to the gods above the clouds, Carole stopped him. "Lance, dear. We have bigger TV cameras watching us than you or I ever used on our OWN independent productions. We only have one more day to be professionals. Then we can be…"

"Shooting something easy," the UCLA grad continued. "Some kind of movie where everyone doesn't act like it's about life and death. For Christ's sake, it's just a movie."

"Yeah," Carole said, knowing fully well that there was more on line here than money or egos. More than who gets to go on Letterman to promote the flick, and who has to do 30 minutes with Charlie Rose or Bill Moyers on PBS.

David put Harry through the blocking, being sure that the most profound dialogue for sound check was "one, two, three, check," and "I wanna get a boink tonight, okay, check, check, check."

Lance liked what he saw. "I can work with it," he kept repeating, as he looked at David's blocking. It was the best compliment Lance ever gave a director. He even gave Harry a "looking real good, kid," a fatherly "way to go," and a solid "hit it on the nail."

Hitting it on the nail was exactly what was required for the last scene, a face-off duel between the main character, 'Rex', and the Illuminati chairman of the board. Emotional stopgaps were off for the scene that would be the ideological Super Bowl of all time. Good vs. evil. Right vs. wrong. Life vs. death. Freedom vs. slavery.

The Professor hardly recognized Harry under the blood makeup. But he recognized the eyes of the actor, so engrossed in preparing for his role that even the pigeons kept their distance.

Most of the winged creatures found a haven, maybe a home, with the Professor. As always, they chose the right piece of paper to lay their excremental commentary upon. "A TV Guide," Professor Jack commented to them, while preparing for the shoot-out of shoot-outs.

Jack fed his avian companions the last of his food, then read on. "'Conspiracy Buster' Renewed for the fall.' This is the one where non-Hollywood writers send in their best anti-conspiracy stories, ideas, and experiences, then get them rewritten by drama pros who know how to make hard reality into watchable fiction. 'The Producer, Sonny Luther, was inspired by Oliver Stone and decided to bring in The Sixth Estate to keep the system honest.'" Jack laughed under his cold breath. "Sonny Luther worked for the CIA, so did his father. Everyone who submits a script gets, at the very least, a signed picture of Oliver Stone, a note of thanks, and a wiretap on their phone for the next decade. If the ideas get into the final draft script, then on the air, they get invited into the family. An offer NO one can refuse."

The Professor took a long pause. Again, the doubts about it all came into place. To save Harry, he would kill the most powerful men and women in the world. To save the truth, he was prepared to kill Harry. To preserve the integrity of history, he would have to kill himself.

Professor Jack worked out the scenarios in his battle-weary head. Twenty bullets could go into twelve Illuminati CEOs very easily if they turned against Harry. If Harry turned against the letter, or spirit, of "Code to Die For," one of the bullets would go into his heart. There might be another Gen-X kid somewhere with enough grit, fire, and connection to life to follow through. And there was always the book, already written and ready for underground presses everywhere. If Harry died for the book, what better publicity? And how ironic, if Harry was rewarded for cowardice, at the last moment, with a promotion to being a Messiah gunned down in the service of the new International People's Revolution?

But the pigeons would live. So would the truth, even if there was no one left to live it anymore. That would be the worst-case scenario. And, true to form, the off-set B-plot was evolving to that conclusion.

A tired old cowboy and a short-haired street-whore-turned-revolutionary snuck up to the barricade. The cowboy slipped the police lieutenant a fistful of twenties. The young woman gave him a smile, an inviting stroke on his rough cheek, and a hotel room key. The mismatched pair was allowed entry, a front row view, complete with Special Visitor passes that even Patrolmen couldn't get.

The Professor had seen Ross's eyes only once, on rugged individualist "Marlboro Man" posters, which hovered over so many non-rugged conformists on Madison Avenue, Pennsylvania Avenue, and Rodeo Drive. The woman next to him looked like Leona, at least around the eyes. Why was Ross so reluctant to accept a loving hug from her? Why were his attentions on a security guard's horse, and the rifle so openly displayed in the saddlebag? He already looked well armed, like those CIA operatives with terminal cancer. The kind with a big debt to pay off, or a life sentence in prison commuted to an honorable death. The kind who walked into the middle of a village at noon, then exited into oblivion by 12:01, along with the village itself.

An unexpected enemy was the last thing Professor Jack, or Harry, needed right now, but uninformed friends were even more dangerous.

CHAPTER 39

"Camera, speed, in five, four," the A.D. yelled out.

"And, action!!!." David interjected to steal the two vital seconds Harry would need to prepare for the scene.

The Cadillac zoomed onto the set at full speed. 'Rex' made a run for it, then fell on the pavement.

"The car's gonna hit him," Carole said to David. "That wasn't in the script."

"It is now, " David said, with a wide grin.

"There's no way to escape from that alley, David. The stunt men and Harry think there's a getaway ladder, but it's not there. Rex is gonna…."

"Finish the scene alive. He's a lot more versatile than you think."

From above, Professor Jack assessed the situation from behind the sights of a rifle. Too many steel walls in the way, and a rotating ramp that kept turning on every shot. The alternative of shooting David was out of the question. Besides, Davy boy had already arranged for bulletproof glass to be placed behind his back and on his sides.

In a flash of the moment, Professor Jack remembered that it was the same kind of glass the Secret Service used in 1963, except for that fatal day in Dallas, when the country lost a President and inherited a lie.

Leona let out a blood-curdling scream. "Harry!!!" Studio guards grabbed her. Before the Illuminati security plainclothes could apprehend her cowboy "uncle," he had disappeared into the crowd. A crowd control cop discreetly asked if anyone had seen his horse.

The Cadillac zoomed in, even closer. Harry's career was about to begin, and end, with the biggest flesh vs. metal clash ever filmed.

"David," Carole warned. "Let Rex die and…."

"It's your responsibility. You wanted to be a production manager, Carole."

She opened her mouth to scream. It was silenced by the barrel of a revolver in the small of her back.

"If Rex dies, David."

"He'll get what he's been after his entire life, Carole."

David punctuated the conversation with a grin. Carole prepared for the lose-lose scenario of her life. A kid was going to die because of a movie, she thought, because of money. Human flesh is worth less than pieces of green paper. The global logic of it all hit home, finally.

Harry somehow found his way up to his feet again. The ramp is elevated. Run up, and it was a chance for life. Run down, and flesh would meet steel. Jump down, and skull bones would break against concrete.

The black multinational hearse rushed up the runway, slipping into what seemed like sixth gear. Harry looked over at David. All cameras were on, all operators cued in to some escape route that Harry would find, or create.

Harry saw in David's face the only thing that could save him. The "you're not good enough to be one of us" sneer, the stare of condescension that Harry always submitted to, or evaded. The bargain always bought him survival. At that moment, Harry realized that he was a survivor.

"Fuck you!!!" Harry yelled to the hooded driver, then to every camera lens in sight. "Fuck you all!!" he directed at David.

For the Cadillac, five seconds left to contact. Harry's life would depend on what happened here. One set of eyes hung on Harry. Harry stared directly back into them.

"You are fuckin dead, Dad. I've just fuckin killed you!!," he screamed, in a voice that was all Harry and no Rex. Harry tore off his Latex mask and tossed it at the windshield. He ripped open the designer shirt and picked up a ten-foot pole, insistent that if chrome hit flesh, the beam would penetrate the windshield.

In the infinity of his last living moments, he stood naked to the world and to the man who had terrorized him for the last two years.

Jack felt his most painful emotion; uselessness. Not unless he could bank 45 caliber shells against three steel backdrops.

The cameras rolled. David smirked. Carole felt his gun poke her vagina. The car screeched to the left, crashing into a pillar.

Hardball was shocked. How could superstar Rex be Harry? How could Harry stand up to anyone? And how dare he stage the final battle between them in public?

"Kill that motherfucker now!" Hardball blasted out, pistol in hand, an army of thugs behind him.

"Your turn to die this time," Harry countered, with quiet conviction. He knew it would be a prelude to a run. A flat-out charge, or full-bore retreat, or both at once. Could human feet dodge lead-alloy bullets? Had he hung with Professor Jack long enough to inherit the old coot's protection from bullets, disease, and other insults that killed or crippled mortal humans? The answer unequivocally was "no." He still wasn't crazy enough to be that protected.

Harry ran toward high ground, a place of higher visibility for whatever would happen next. Flying pieces of lead flew out of Hardball's gun, and from the security force leased to him by the Illuminati. Ladders broke, railings fell, and roofs collapsed, but not a scratch to Harry.

The crowd below cheered. Carole breathed a sigh of relief. David nodded his finger. From the other side of the ramp emerged two other vehicles, 451 sedans armed with deathmobile chrome.

A thousand emotions battled for Harry's soul, shots from the alley, a whinnying horse, and a rebel yell. Shots from the roof dispersed the crowd.

"Cut!" Carole yelled. "Cut!!!"

David waved his hands. "No. Keep rolling. Keep rolling." He turned to Carole. "I can use the background noise, and you can use the rest."

Carole was escorted off the set. "You're finished," she said, as a prophesy and a prayer.

"And so is he," David said to himself, while eyeing Hardball. Twenty Illuminati guns took Hardball's guards captive.

Hardball had never been more out of control, and never in a place where it was more inappropriate. "Harry. I'll fuckin' kill you. I'll fucking kill you, too, David. I'll fuckin' kill you . . ."

"Shut him up, he's not one of us anymore," David said to a blue-eyed Nordic gentleman in a tweed jacket. Hans Webster was rumored to have been the unofficial chair of the Illuminati board, a position that rotated every three months.

The Professor recognized Webster very well. It had been thirty years, but he still looked like the Prussian-Anglo uppercrust Neonazi he had always been. His blonde hair had turned white and had thinned a bit, but his stare and manner were still the same, autocratic. Webster was pure Illuminati, Old Guard Rigid and New Order cruel, all combined into one package.

One bullet from Jack could end it for Webster, or perhaps do something different. Harry's feet violated the laws of physics. His leaps and jumps astounded even the stuntmen. Behind him, the cars, approaching like vultures on a mouse that somehow had crossed into the harshest desert created by the hand of God or man.

Leona was impressed, even proud. "That's my brother," she boasted to the guards who were taking her to what would be a very ugly death. "That's my fuckin' brother up there!!!."

Webster came into the Professor's sight. He could get off one shot. One shot to kill the devil incarnate. But what of Harry? Does a General have an obligation to the mission or his men? If you could kill Hitler or save one Jewish child, which would you do with your last bullet?

The Professor fired. A bullet took out the first car, then the second. Screeching and crashing, everything got on film. Only four cars are left to attack Harry. Only three bullets are left in the Professor's gun.

"Cut!!!" David yelled out. Then, a single bullet silenced the chaos.

It came from a lone horseman. Ross Cuthand had put one round soundly into the intercom system that made David's meek voice sound so big. David would have to speak on his own. But no one was listening. The spectacle was too great.

Webster smiled. He liked the confusion. "The weak are being weeded out. So we can inherit the strong."

Ross turned the horse around, aimed the police rifle, then fired. The first bullet nicked Hardball in the groin, inches from his most overrated and overused organ.

Leona screamed out, "Daddy!!!" She had dreamed about seeing Hardball Harold castrated. He had done it to so many other people. But she was Daddy's little girl. No matter that she had spent six months being his personal whore. "Noo!!!" she screamed. It echoed prayer and battlecry.

"Come to Daddy. Daddy still loves you," Hardball bellowed out to Leona. "Shoot the bitch when she gets to the catering truck," he whispered out the side of his mouth to his henchmen. "And make it look like she got shot by that geek up on the roof. My boy 'Rex' might have to rethink his loyalties after his buddy Professor Jack offs his sister."

Ross watched with an eye that could put everything in slow motion and not miss a single beat. He saw the Professor aiming at Hardball's head. One shot now, in the absence of the car chases below, would give away Jack's position. With every frame, the slow-mo made for horror-scream nightmare got worse. Leona fell under her father's spell again, in the blink of an eye. She ran towards Hardball, twenty yards away from losing her soul, ten from losing her life. The hit would be well-choreographed, Ross intuited. Leona, Harry, and most probably Professor Jack would be killed at the same time, Hardball getting the credit for trying to save all of them.

Ross galloped to his best vantage point, then took aim. "One more round," he thought to himself. "Better make them think that I got a thousand, and that I'm more superhero than anything these Hollywood wimps ever even imagined."

Webster discreetly nodded his finger. Leona was allowed to comfort Hardball. David was escorted back to the director's chair and forced to watch the rest of the scene.

Leona hugged her father, then felt a thunderbolt that ended life as she knew it. The bullet went straight into Hardball's hard head. A direct hit.

"Excellent work," one of Webster's associates commented to Lance.

"David writes the words, I just get the pictures," Lance said, with a modesty befitting his cinemagraphic abilities. He looked over to the director's chair. David sat quietly, under discreet but very heavy guard. "Did Davy boy yell cut yet?" Lance asked the black-haired, Semitic-looking Illuminati rep, who looked half-banker and half-rock star.

"I don't think so," board member John Bernstein-Smith commented.

Ross galloped in to sweep Leona away from the armed guards, with the help of cover, and stray shots from an unknown assailant on the roof. Bullets and manure, rocks and garbage served to give the Lone Ranger the diversion he needed. But the horse was willing, the crowd was pleased, and everyone on the wrong side of the morality line was scared shitless of the thunder that could come out of the barrel of the real-life Clint Eastwood, bringing romantic adventure into the most jaded city in North America.

Then, the buzz of a motorcycle. Harry grabbed his own equine beast-a 250 cc Honda, which he mounted like a 1200 cc Harley. Facing him, three deathmobiles, manned by extras who had real guns. Behind him, a line of rebel ghost spirits goes back to the Alamo, and beyond.

Harry grabbed a set of twelve rods from the ground. Taking them up like spears, he began to sing his death song and life song.

"This rod is for the contribution of Illuminati member 3. Ivan Federoff. The Bosnian conflict, the Peruvian civil war, the Chinese anthrax epidemic." He chucked the spear into the generator. A surge of lights flashed and burned bright and pure. Every news camera on site got it all: light, sound, and full angle.

"Fuck, we got light. We got some light," Lance said. "Keep rolling."

Webster rose up, stared indignantly, then raised his hand. Before the all-too-often used "sig heil" position could be reached, Harry took another rod into hand.

"This one is for board member ten, Kyoto Kamura. The Angolan famine, the Tanzanian holocaust." The rod-turned-lance flung in the air and plunged into one of the deathmobiles. The operators of the mechanical beast left it just before the gas tank blew.

The Professor smiled. The cameras rolled, filming every stride of the cowboy rescuing the damsel in distress, galloping down the Avenue of the Americas. Catching every frame of Harry's last stand.

Harry's next lance went into Deathmobile Two, through the windshield. Another board member was named, her role in the economic collapse of three Latin American companies and half of Africa was clearly made public. Uneventful, but visually interesting, Lance thought, as he directed camera 6 to stay with the action, and camera 10 to reload another roll of film ASAP.

Webster stood up, grabbed a rifle, and aimed it.

Harry turned around. "And for Jack Kennedy Webster," he said, turning around. "Führer of the year." Harry tossed the rod up, aiming it with the precision of a spirit prepared to die, and so connected to life that it redefined everything and everyone around him.

The rod hit its mark - a foot in front of Webster's feet. Harry stripped naked in front of him.

"CUT!!!" Harry yelled up to the cameras. "But not my doink. I still can use that."

The crowd laughed. David sulked. A few powerful people who hid amongst the commoner crowd disappeared. Maybe they would change careers, identities, or lifestyles. Or maybe not.

"This is my movie," Webster announced.

"Yeah, but it's my show," Harry countered. "Roll, speed, and action!"

Taken in by what he still thought was the most impressive piece of action-adventure in his career, Lance signaled his people to roll. No one but the insiders knew the real stories, and none would reveal the code to anyone outside the "in-the-know" circle.

Carole remained the only one who didn't know that "Code to Die For" was being played out for keeps. Informing anyone that it was not fantasy would get her killed, and Carole still valued living in obscurity over dying in glory.

"Sig Heil, to you and your fucking fourth Reich," Harry shouted to Webster. "I guess this means that I get to be one of the beautiful people, now. I'm strong, young, and the chicks like me. I'm a fuckin' winner. Right?"

Up on the roof, the Professor heard footsteps coming his way. "They got Oswald because of triangulation," he thought. "Appropriate that they should get me like that." But in the forefront of the Professor's mind was still the truth. Harry had been possessed by a strange beast, and all of this had been to destroy the Illuminati, not Webster. Could Harry be bought at the last minute? What was the displaced Gen-X'er really made of?

Webster reached into his pocket. Harry backed away. He wrapped a loincloth around his genitalia, then grabbed another rod, a short one with a sharp point.

"On the count of five, Herr Webster?" Harry started the countdown. "One, two, three . . ."

"Four," Webster interrupted. He tossed Harry a purse from his pocket, a leather pouch with gold Medieval engravings. "Go ahead, open it. If you have the courage to."

As Harry glanced upon the offering, he felt the fire in him extinguish for a moment. His human fire couldn't hold up against the medallion, which seemed so bright, complexly crafted, and powerful.

"I need a close-up," Lance yelled out.

Harry kept the medal close to him, denying everyone a view, even the Professor.

"The spell is real, Harold," Webster said, with a tone more fatherly than authoritative. "It's called truth. Enlightenment. Peace. You've earned it."

"A Masonic symbol, surrounded by some other shit," Harry commented. "What is all this other shit, Webster?"

"A tradition that you could put right. That you must make right, kill me, if you have to. But that, and what it stands for. It belongs to you." Webster extended his hand to Harry.

Harry melted down. He imagined himself with power. Rested. Peaceful. "And my friends, Webster?"

"Safe. Sound. Happy, if they want to be. We'll provide them with all they need."

The stairwell to the Professor's hideout turned abruptly silent. Maybe the words were real, the promises guaranteed.

"And what will you give ME?" Harry asked. "What's in it for me?"

"Anything you want, Harold."

Harry pondered a moment, a final recheck before the critical decision. Logic, intuition, and common sense would all have to be consulted and integrated. "There's just one thing, Webster."

"What, Harold?"

"I don't like being called Harold." Harry unwrapped his loincloth. "This medal is a little tarnished. I think it needs a cleaning."

Harry pulled out the four-inch evidence of his manhood and proceeded to wash the prized Illuminati membership badge with his urine. "Get a close-up of this, Lance. With lots of background." Lance accommodated. Harry tossed the medal back into Webster's face. "Cut. And that's a rap." Harry was consumed by terror and bliss. He called it "freedom."

The crowd went mad. The chant of "Harry!!!" could be heard from Battery Park to Yonkers, but not so loud as from the roof.

Jack rose up, rifle in hand. "Harrry!!!" he screamed out, made all the more terrifying by a bone-dry throat. Squad team rifle barrels focused on Jack's chest, but another executioner had first dibs. Jack's heart took a final beat, hard and intense, then stopped.

The Professor's rebel yelp was silenced by one last gasp, then a ten-story fall. With a puff of smoke, a flash of light, and a thud that echoed in the inner ear like thunder, it was all over. Or was it?

CHAPTER 40

"The biggest boom to bust sensation since 'Howard the Duck'," the Times said. "Hollywood has found yet another way to turn good money into tax-write off losses, topping 'Waterworld', 'Heaven's Gate', and 'Living in America'. After 'Code to Die For', if David Deitrick can get a job as a movie usher after this over-the-top box office flop, it will be an overestimation of financial potential," the Wall Street Journal movie critic commented. The Village Voice was the worst. "It took Dustin Hoffman and Warren Beatty three movies to live down 'Ishtar'. It will take new superstar 'Harry Rex' three lifetimes to live down his writing, acting, and music debut in 'Code to Die For'."

"Okay," Harry said to Leona. "So I should have got a real orchestra to play the background music. Maybe R & B doesn't work for my flick. Maybe I should have gotten someone else to do the score wall-to-wall."

With the Oregon ocean air in her face, the Cascade Mountains at her back, Leona continued the painful read. "There's as much subtlety in 'Code to Die For' as there is in Howard Stern's radio show."

"At least I'm in good company," Harry commented, while feeding a wild gull which was too proud to come down for food, and too smart to make himself dependent on human garbage as his source of nutrients.

"Harry, it's only been a month," Leona pointed out.

"And the movie is already on video release." Harry reflected on everything that had happened since the shoot. Barely a month ago, he was in the middle of the most powerful political struggle in the world. Now he was more concerned with making sure that his second-hand twenty-foot "yacht," PT-109A, had enough resined varnish on its hull to keep it seaworthy.

"You got it on the record, Harry. Without any rewrites. And you got your fifteen minutes." Leona sewed up the rest of the mainsail.

"Yeah. I got a fucking underground audience now," Harry said with the cynicism of a man far older than his years, even older than the Professor.

"An underground audience is the best kind, Harry. It can't be bought. And it's always there."

"You think so?"

"I don't know, Harry. Do you?"

Harry looked at the PT109 plate on the boat. "You think Professor Jack was at the premiere? The Enquirer says he died from spontaneous combustion. The Village Voice said he was fucking a CIA-IRA operative. The goddamn Times didn't mention him at all. We ALL blew the lid on the biggest fuckin' conspiracy in history a month ago, and now we're using K-Mart paint on a second-hand boat, worried about how we're gonna get rent money again. The Illuminati officially dissolved. But Webster is still alive."

"So are we, Harry."

"Not all of us, Leona." Harry's glee turned instantly to sorrow. He felt the pain as much as Leona did.

"At least Mickey got to see you on tape with Hollywood big shots. The doctors said he recognized you. He died in his sleep. The hospital said it was a brain tumor."

"Yeah, right." Harry's grief instantly turned into rage.

"Harry. It's over. Brain tumors happen to people who get hit in the head when they're real little, then turn mentally retarded when they get bigger. He was dying before I got . . . ya know . . . reacquainted with 'Daddy'." The words hurt her mouth, choking in her throat. "And Mickey's brain was gone before you met old man Kennedy."

"President Kennedy!!!" Harry protested. "Professor. Jack. Or Professor Jack. Professor Asshole. Fuckin' Professor Spaceman. NO one calls him old man."

"No one did," a calm voice said from a high vantage point. Ross Cuthand looked as much a warrior in his biker Viking helmet as he did a cowboy in a well-seasoned Stetson.

"Your beard looks different today. Bigger. Wilder," Leona commented.

"Testosterone and no sleep'll do that to ya," Ross volleyed back. He slapped the top layer of road dust off his black chaps and parked his new 1200 cc steed on the pier. He unzipped the inner compartment in the black leather and retrieved an envelope. "Your inheritance, Harry. You sure you want it?"

"Yeah, I'm fuckin' sure," Harry said, his hand shaking as he reached for the envelope and opened it. "Dust to dust. Ashes to ashes. Is this all there was?"

"I scraped the ground myself. Some of your friends didn't get consumed by that fire; their bodies burned up in it."

"Bet it's his dick." Harry never smirked with so much reverence. "Jack never used it. His brain burned up first. His eyes probably went next. But his dick. He never used it. Unlike some of us." Harry turned to Ross.

"Things happen. Unfulfilled passions and reproducible accidents," Ross replied.

Leona reached her hand out to Ross's. She brought it to her belly. "A son, I think. When we exchanged souls in the hotel room in Oklahoma, you were thinking 'son'. So was I."

Ross cracked a smile, nearly shattering the Spartan rigidity of his ever-in-control sunbaked face.

Harry cleared his throat. "So. Ya gonna marry her? You bang up my sister, ya gotta do right by her. It's tradition."

"Harry, your sister's a very non-traditional person. And a very special one." No moment between man, woman, and unborn child could have been more silently and subtly "loving."

"Fuck this noise, Ross," Harry slurred out in his most ethnic Brooklynese. "I don't give a shit if it's a fucking tree in the goddamn woods with a naked, fag, Buddhist priest reading a porno Hallmark card. We're gonna have a fuckin' wedding!!"

The moment of love under tension was broken by a herd of mechanical beasts. The cliff above abounded with rebel bikers, all on regulation 1400 cc Harley choppers. The Portland chapter of the Hells Angels hadn't gone riding in full colors and full force since the biker gang wars of the eighties forced the clubs to go underground. With the demise of Hardball Harold Diamantis' iron hand on the mob, it was all up for grabs again. The bikers' day in the sun had come back, and they wouldn't surrender it again. The 'one percenters' would take care of business 100% of the time.

"They're my bodyguards," Ross related to Leona.

"My old friends," she added, extreme caution in her now wide-open eyes. "I shouldn't have called them."

"Why, Leona? I'm a hero. The man who gunned down Hardball Harold. In open combat, against a hundred to one odds."

"They'll find you out, Ross."

"They already know I was a cop and an enforcer for the Diamantis organization. What else can they find out, Leona?"

"That under all the dark and ugly sides of you, you're a good person. You don't enjoy evil the way they do. One day, they'll kill you for it."

"Yeah. But right now, they're the most reliable posse an honorable outlaw can get. We still need them, Leona. For the cause. Illuminatis pop up when no one's watching, or nobody cares."

"Fuck the Cause, Ross," Leona let out. "And fuck the Illuminati. I need you. And so does your son. Tell him, Harry."

Harry looked downward, guilty of having to be himself in a very tough role.

Leona would not be kept silent by male bondage or even human logic. "Great, Ross. So and Harry goes up into the mountains with your kid. Brother and sister raise a baby. They'll think we're from fuckin' Arkansas."

The biker battle horns from the cliff heralded Ross back to his warrior post.

"One more minute," Ross yelled up to them.

The bikers jeered and whistled. One more quickie boink with his old lady, and then the cowboy would lead them back to their rightful places, as drifters who answered to no one.

Leona was less than impressed at the gesture.

Ross drew her close, lowering his voice. "Leona. I still prefer motorcycles with hoofs. High desert anything to concrete anywhere. And real people to powerful people."

"So why are you going back with those bikers? So you can fight with the new Illuminati?"

"If I do this right, fast and alone, there won't be any new Illuminati."

"If you believe that, Ross, then you're as fucking stupid as Jack was," Harry interjected, while glancing at the ashes left of the Professor's bones, measuring up to less than one tenth of the mass of a normal human body.

Perhaps the "spontaneous combustion" theory of his demise was true. Mass did convert to energy, Jack's last statement, his final defiance of death. Still, some ashes had to be left behind for those unfortunate enough to continue in the land of the "living."

Harry flung the tarp of the emergency lifeboat into the water. Finally, it was time.

"A Viking funeral," Harry related, as he put the ashes into the vessel, substantially modified from its geometrically 20th-century design. "The stern has a dragon head. The starboard side has these shields of all the Presidents. The port side has his family on it. Bobby. Rose. His lawyer turned-Yuppoid kid, John Junior. Even his father, Joe, the self-righteous motherfucker."

Harry flung the boat into the water, then the ashes on top.

Leona looked into Ross's eyes. The truth and feeling of the matter overcame any logic.

"Leona," Ross said, with the finality of a dying man, or perhaps one in transition to a higher life plane. "What kind of father would I be if I made our son live in the kind of world WE had to spend our lives dying in?"

"And what kind of mother would you think I was if I let you abandon him?"

Harry broke into song. "Camelot, yes, Camelot, my boy . . ." The Richard Harris version, belted out with the sun setting over the Pacific horizon. Harry made himself sing the words. Ross and Leona watched, knowing it was not their place to join in, but to share the experience in a more profound way.

Harry lit the torch, set the raft ablaze, and pushed it out to sea. He gave voice to his dreams, hopes, and love. "Where once it never rained till after sundown. By eight, the morning fog had disappeared. Don't let it be forgot. That once there was a spot. One fleeting glimpse of glory that was known as . . . Camelot!!!!"

The outward tide took Professor Jack's Presidential ship beyond the Western Horizon, where it melded with Infinity. The tear from Harry's starboard eye fell into the ocean, reigniting the entire world.